Travelers
A Zimbell House
Anthology

Travelers

A Zimbell House Anthology

ZIMBELL HOUSE
PUBLISHING
UNION LAKE, MICHIGAN

© 2015 Zimbell House Publishing, LLC
Cover Design by The Book Planners
www.TheBookPlanners.com

Published in the United States by
Zimbell House Publishing LLC
http://www.ZimbellHousePublishing.com
All Rights Reserved

Print ISBN: 978-1-942818-54-0
Kindle ISBN: 978-1-942818-58-8
Digital ISBN: 978-1-942818-59-5
Trade Paper ISBN: 978-1-945967-53-5
Library of Congress Control Number: 2015921356

First Edition: January/2016
10 9 8 7 6 5 4

ZIMBELL HOUSE PUBLISHING
UNION LAKE, MICHIGAN

Acknowledgements

Zimbell House Publishing would like to thank all those who contributed to this anthology. We selected four voices that best represented our vision.

We would also like to thank our Zimbell House team for all their hard work to bring this project to fruition. A special thank you goes out to The Book Planners for the cover design.

Contents

A Teller of Fortunes

Sammi Cox

I

Astre couldn't remember market day being so busy before, she decided, as she looked about the cobbled square and the adjoining green, both of which were crammed with people, stalls, and entertainers. It reminded Astre of a holiday or a saint's festival, and yet she knew it was neither, nor did she complain at its busyness.

From her little booth next to the river, a stone's throw away from the town bridge, Astre was in a prime location. Her pitch was one of the first those crossing the bridge would see, when they still had coins in their purse and the excitement of market day had yet to wane. The tent was, conversely, one of the last travelers would see as they made their way home, and if, by chance they still had a coin or two to call their own, many of them would not hesitate to cross

Astre's palm in return for hearing what she had to say about their future.

Astre was a fortune teller. She would travel from fair to fair, from market to festival, plying her trade in fortunes and charms. Her reputation was known far and wide, and countless people often sought her out.

Of course, her sort were not always welcome. Sometimes towns would refuse travelers entry, whether or not they could pay the toll to get through the gates or pay the fee for a pitch at the market. Sometimes towns would take their monies before an incensed crowd, no doubt stirred up by those officials who didn't want them there, chased them to beyond the settlement's limits.

Astre was lucky. She had yet to be faced with an angry mob. A few comments here and there were the worst things she had come across, and she thanked the stars for that. She always preferred traveling alone, with no-one but her trusted pony for company. Every now and then, she would meet others on the road and stay with them a day or two, but it was never long before she would take her leave again, off on her solitary path to find enough coins to keep her well-fed and warm.

As a well-attuned woman, she recognized that traveling alone left her vulnerable. Nevertheless, Astre believed it was the fact that she did travel alone that solely ensured she could always gain entry to a town, and therefore, acquire a pitch at the market. What was there to fear from one woman, traveling by herself? How much trouble could she cause? The answer was plenty, but she needn't remind anyone of that.

As Astre sat on her three-legged stool beside her tent, dressed in her brightly colored clothes, she continued to enjoy the lull in her trade. She knew it would not last long - it never did. However, it gave her the opportunity to brew some tea and to eat a little bread and cheese, whilst she continued to watch the market day revelers.

Most seemed happy. The merchants, on the whole, were doing good business; this town was one of the wealthiest in the area so the inhabitants could afford a little indulgence. A group of girls were staring and giggling at a young entertainer. When he had finished his song, he doffed his cap at them and winked cheekily, causing the girls run away blushing. An egg woman, carrying one of the largest baskets Astre had ever seen, was deftly maneuvering through the crowd, calling out her price list as she went. Even when she made a sale, the woman refused to stand still and continued to tout for customers, briefly breaking her rhythm to thank the customer for their purchase.

It was then that Astre spotted someone who did not appear so content with his day. The man was clearly a wealthy merchant; his fine clothes, cut from expensive cloth in the latest fashion, marked him out as such. But he was also bad-tempered. His face was red from shouting, and Astre looked on as he aimed an angry boot at a man lying on the ground. Astre's expression soured; even if the man had done something wrong it was for the town's justice to deal with, no-one else. She looked away, disgusted.

"How much for my fortune?" a voice said, intruding on her thoughts. Never had Astre been more glad of an interruption. She turned around to face the voice, to find one of the girls she had seen watching the jongleur. The fortune teller knew almost instantly what this was about.

"How much do you have?" Astre asked kindly.

"Two pennies," the girl responded shyly, showing her outstretched open palm with the two little coins sitting in it. "Is it enough?"

Astre didn't have the heart to take from the girl; she knew how hard young girls had to work to earn a pittance. From the state of her hand, she could see she was a scullery maid who probably spent the time between getting up early and going to bed late scrubbing cold stone floors.

"I would rather ask a favor in return for revealing your fortune. You keep the coins. Favors are worth so much more," Astre said, with a flair that was often part of her performance.

The girl bit her lip, wondering what this favor could be. She was torn; she wanted her fortune read, but she didn't want to be in the debt of a fortune teller. "What sort of favor?" she finally asked.

"You're from the town, aren't you?" The girl nodded. "You know who bakes the best bread, then?" Again the girl nodded. "Good. I need a fresh loaf to take with me on the road. Go and fetch one for me and I will speak to you of the future when you return. You will have a very big decision to make when you get back. You must choose between the tarot cards, the stones, the crystal ball or the tea leaves. Only then can we see what the future holds."

Astre handed over a few coins and watched the girl disappear off into the crowd. She had no fear that the girl would choose to pocket the few pennies instead of using them to pay for the bread. The girl was desperate to see if a tall, dark, handsome troubadour would soon rescue her from her life of drudgery. Sadly, as was usually the case, the fortune teller knew there was not.

The morning passed very quickly as Astre became inundated by those who wanted to know what good they had to look forward to and if they were unlucky, any evil they might prepare for and perchance avert. The crystal ball was the favored choice for many of those who visited the booth, whilst those who were thirsty or required one of the herbal tonics that Astre often dispensed elected to have their tea leaves read, believing they were getting two things for the price of one.

Afternoon came and went, and the day moved towards evening. The crowd began to thin as did the number of pennies they still had in their pockets. Some traders who had sold all their goods packed up and started the trek to the next town and the next market; others waited until it had been a good while since they had made a sale before joining the snake of traffic thronging the town bridge.

Of course, a good number found themselves lodgings within the town. Many inns and taverns could be found off the market square; some were quite decent, whilst some had a more dubious character.

Astre was not in a rush to leave, but she would be gone before the gatehouse closed it's giant wooden doors at curfew. She was happy to wait until the roads emptied a little; it was easier for her to drive her wagon if the way was clear.

A few stragglers stopped by to spend their last coins prior to heading home for their supper. One man exchanged a thick rasher of bacon for a charm Astre cast on his behalf. Once he left, Astre had the feeling it was time to leave; she had an inbuilt sense that often guided her and it had not failed yet.

Slowly, she packed away her own tent and belongings, put out the small fire she had needed to boil the water for her tea, before hitching the pony to the wagon. Lastly, she checked that her most valuable items, the tools of her trade, the tarot cards, the stones, the crystal ball and the special cup from which she read the tea leaves, were stowed away safely in one of the little cupboards in the back of the wagon. Then she closed the door, which was painted with flowers and magical symbols in a great number of colors, and climbed up into the driver's seat.

It was then that a commotion from near the town bridge caught her attention. A small crowd had gathered, but it wasn't stationary. As it passed the wagon, she could see at its center the merchant she had taken a dislike to earlier. He was holding someone by the scruff of the neck and dragging them off. When they stumbled on the cobblestones, his boot was used to ensure they kept moving.

The merchant must have felt her eyes on him, for he suddenly turned around and looked at her. "Do you have something to say, madam?" he shouted.

Astre knew that she should keep silent, if only for the sake of the poor wretch who was being humiliated at his hands, but she refused to look away. He would not scare her, the bully. The power of her intense stare ensured that he was first to break eye contact, and the crowd moved on.

Clicking her tongue, she gently pulled on one of the reins and the pony started to walk. As Astre took her leave of the town, she waved goodbye to a few familiar faces she recognized but she was not sad to be going. Soon it would be just her and the pony and the clear, open sky from which no trouble could come.

Passing beneath the dark grey, ominous looking archway, she left the town and the bad-tempered merchant behind her. She had an hour or so to find somewhere suitable to stop for the night, before the dark set in. However, try as she might, she could not shake the feeling that she and the merchant would cross paths - and perhaps swords - once more.

II

On leaving the town, Astre took the road that followed the river. She had passed this way on a number of occasions and knew of a suitable place to make camp for a day or two. It was on the edge of the woods, a little way from the road.

When she reached it, she allowed the pony to roam whilst she set up her tent. Rather than pitching it as she would at a fair, she attached the canvas to a couple of trees and propped up the top with a number of timber struts. This provided shelter on two sides but kept the front and back open as well as giving it a sloping roof. Should it rain, the water would simply run off, but there would be enough room within it for the pony to keep dry.

Once the tent was up, she called to the pony, whom she tethered on a long lead to a tree. Then she brushed her down before she fired up the little stove in the wagon. There was no need for her to light a fire out of doors that evening. Soon the kettle was whistling, and Astre was warming her hands with a cup of hot tea. Once her thirst was sated, she inspected her fresh loaf of bread - the best that the town had, she remembered, groaning at the indulgence. Asking the girl to fetch it was the first errand that came into her head. She would never usually spend so much on a loaf but, she considered, at least, it made the girl think she had earned her free fortune.

Astre cooked the thick rasher of bacon she had acquired in a frying pan on top of the stove. She was pleased to see that it was wrapped in a good layer of fat, which she cooked off and put to one side, planning to use it in a stew or soup later in the week. She would not waste it.

Sitting in the doorway of the wagon, her legs dangling off the edge, she ate her meal of bread and bacon, washing it down with a second cup of tea. The view from her vantage point was spectacular. In the dying light she could see the curving bend of the river to one side of her, and to the other the lengthening shadows of the forest, that crept nearer and nearer as the night settled in.

Astre did not fear the forest or the dark. She had heard the tales of wood shades - spirits of men and women who had died in the forest as outlaws. But the dead did not scare her. Her charms she knew would keep the curious wood shades away, and much more besides.

With her shawl wrapped around her shoulders and her long, wavy dark hair hanging loosely down her back, Astre grabbed an apple and went to feed the pony. Then she walked a little beneath the clear, night sky. The moon and stars were out now. And, she noted, that for the time being at least, the weather would remain dry.

Eventually, her mind turned to reflect on the market. *Trade had been good, very good,* she acknowledged. Although she had not counted the coins she had collected - one didn't need to tempt the hand of fate, or a thief - she knew she had made enough money to see her through the month. This was a very rare occurrence indeed. Usually, the fees she would take at a market or fair could last her a week, two if she was careful.

On the one hand, she was pleased. She would not need to rush on to the next town in order to sell fortunes to ensure both she and the pony were kept warm and fed. And yet, it was tempered by the thought that if too much good luck came her way, something would follow to bring the little world she inhabited back into balance.

As soon as the idea crossed her mind, the image of the angry merchant appeared before her eyes. Astre sighed. The man was trouble; it was obvious from the confident swagger of his walk. He thought he was somebody; somebody others should notice and recognize. He had a high opinion of himself, and he would not have taken the challenging look Astre had given him lightly.

Nevertheless, she was not sorry she hadn't looked away. Walking back to the wagon, and to her bed, she simply said to herself, "Should I meet him, I will deal with him. I will take him as I find him, and no more. And if our paths are not destined to cross, I shall count myself blessed indeed!"

III

Astre slept well in her bed in the wagon. It was surprisingly comfy and well-furnished for a caravan. Along one side was her bed, which also served as a couch, when the need arose. It was not often that she entertained those who sought their fortune in the wagon, but it was not unheard of, especially when she was on the road. The bed was hollow and could be lifted up to reveal a large storage box. The small cupboard tucked away at the bottom of the bed held her most valuable possessions: her money box and the tools with which she could reveal the future. Above the bed was a long shelf where she kept a handful of books - she could both read and write, which surprised many - as well as a number of small baskets which housed her dried herbs. Those still drying were hanging in bunches from the ceiling. Hooks, nails, and pegs could be found in every available space, and a great array of items including dish clothes, mugs, saucepans, paintings, and charms filled the walls. To anyone else, the wagon would have looked to be in perpetual chaos, but Astre knew that everything she owned had its right and proper place, and she had never once lost anything.

There was more light than one imagined inside the caravan, thanks to the two large windows placed opposite each other in the center of the two longest wooden walls.

Matching heavy curtains ensured that no draught made it inside, and the brightly painted exterior shutters when closed, kept out the worst of the inclement weather.

In the corner furthest away from the door, on the other side of the bed, was the stove, which served as a heat source as well as an oven. When the hot plate on top of the stove was cold, Astre liked to place a wide dish of flowers, herbs, nuts, pine cones and anything else she had come across on it to help brighten the already colorful room. The remaining space was taken up by a blanket box which doubled as a bench, next to which was a small table. The table could be extended should she wish it, to allow one person to sit on the bench on one side, and another to sit on the bed on the other.

And this was Astre's home.

That morning, Astre decided that it would be a good time to do a little spring cleaning and to catch up on her chores. She wasn't planning on moving on for at least another day and she was content in this little corner, on the edge of the forest. First, she took her laundry down to the river to wash it. Once it was clean, she spread it out over the bushes and trees that were basking in the warm sunshine. Then she swept out the interior of the wagon, dusted every nook and cranny, brushed down the outside of the caravan and scrubbed the stove.

When she was finished, the sun was at its peak. Using up the last of her vegetables and the fat from the bacon she had saved the night before, she rustled up a stew for her supper and began to cook it over a very low heat. By the time she sat down to eat it that evening, it would have thickened up to an almost soup-like consistency. Then she took a thick slice of bread and cheese, a mug of ale and went to sit on her stool in the sun.

The hard work of the morning had driven from her mind all ill thoughts from the previous day. And yet, now as she sat still, relaxing, they came back to her. With a sigh, she tried to push them away, but they persisted. Why they were so determined to make themselves known to her, Astre was unsure. It was perplexing, but above all, she found it an annoying distraction from the peace and tranquility that she had found. Stubbornly, she forced her mind to think about how she was going to spend her afternoon, as she tried to enjoy her lunch.

She was about half way through her repast when she heard the trundling sound of another cart on the road, accompanied by a horse's hooves clipping the ground. For the moment, the edge of the forest obscured her view, so she could only hear the approaching wagon. In the moments before it came into sight, she got a sudden sinking feeling in her stomach. She put her plate to one side; she had lost her appetite.

Then the cart was clear of the cover and Astre groaned. It wasn't that she recognized the horse nor the cart; they were both unfamiliar to her. However, she immediately knew the face of the pompous man who held the reins.

And what's more, he recognized her.

IV

The merchant guided his horse off the road and made towards Astre's wagon. Astre sipped at her ale, watching his approach. She guessed he had passed the night in the town, only taking his leave of it after he had breakfasted that morning. She wondered why he was heading in her direction. *Was it to speak with me about yesterday?*

As he got closer, she could hear him whistling a tuneless ditty to himself. He seemed to be in high spirits. When he was a dozen or so paces away, he called his horse to a halt. "Good afternoon, Fortune Teller," he said in a friendly tone, all traces of the animosity she had heard in his voice the day before gone.

"Good afternoon, Merchant."

"I saw you at the market yesterday, did I not, selling your fortunes and charms?"

"Yes, you did," Astre replied, thinking to herself that he knew very well he had seen her.

"And did you find trade to be good there?" he asked, jumping down from his cart. It was piled high with stout, wooden boxes, all of which had heavy duty locks keeping them secure.

"I did. It was a good day and most of the people were kind and gracious."

"Kind and gracious?" he scoffed. "Fools with too many coins in their purses than they know what to do with!" He laughed.

Astre didn't like his manner, nor his sense of humor. "You found trade good there too, then," she said dryly.

"I did. I did. Made a pretty penny, I did. As I said, fools. Don't like to barter much, that town. I managed to charge double what I usually get for my goods. So yes, yesterday was a good day."

A momentary pause opened up in the conversation. "Is there something I could be helping you with?" Astre ventured. She tried not to appear rude, especially as the man's ill-temper had improved dramatically and he himself was being extremely cordial. Nevertheless, she did not want him to stay too long; she didn't believe he would make great company over a prolonged period, and she had so been enjoying her little break in the meadow between the forest and the river.

"As a matter of fact, yes. I want to hear my fortune."

Astre groaned inwardly. *How long before the man's mood changed?* she wondered. Not everyone appreciated hearing what Astre had to say, and many of them did not understand that even when her predictions were unfavorable, they at least had the opportunity to mitigate disaster once they knew it was coming their way. "Are you sure, sir? I can only speak the truth, and not all are amenable to it."

"I know very well what it is that I want. I want to have my fortune told to me, and I want you to do it. Now. As for the truth, I know I have nothing to fear from it. So, let's begin, shall we?"

Astre finished her ale and then stood up. She had warned him, there was nothing else for it. He wanted his fortune, and she would reveal it.

V

Astre returned to the wagon to place her plate and mug within and retrieve the items she needed to work the merchant's reading. He followed her and made to step up into the wagon, earning himself a reproving look from the fortune teller. He had not been invited into her home. "You may wait without until I am ready," she called out, sharply. Originally she had intended to read for him in the tent, but the booth was not set up for readings. It would be far easier for her to work in the wagon, and in so doing would bring the reading to a swifter conclusion.

Quickly she extended her little table and covered it with a cloth that she had embroidered small stars onto. Then she went to her little cupboard and pulled out her tarot cards, stones, crystal ball and teacup, before laying them out on the table. Once this was completed, she drew the curtains and lit one of the two lamps that were suspended from the ceiling. From the flames, she set alight a bunch of tightly-bound herbs, which she put out almost immediately and proceeded to waft the heavily-scented smoke around the room.

Finally, when Astre was satisfied that all was ready, she stood in the doorway. "You may now come in." She indicated for him to sit on the bench which creaked beneath him, as she took her own seat opposite him on the bed.

He gazed at the items laid out on the table. But, he was getting ahead of himself. "First you must cross my palm with coin, Merchant. Then I shall reveal what your future has in store for you."

"Do you think I have managed to make my way in the world by parting with my money before I have received what I have bought with it?" the merchant laughed. "Of course not. That would be a bad businessman's way - a poor businessman's way. And I am neither," he boomed heartily. "A canny merchant, I am, with good, sound business sense. I shall hand over payment once I have heard what you have to tell me."

"Surely, by the same token, if I should agree to that, I would be making a poor business decision. Besides, that is not how things are done. What's to say that you will pay me once I have finished speaking? What guarantee do I have?"

The merchant pursed his lips. "I understand what you are saying. And so, I shall put my coins - your fee - on the table here, between us," he said, placing a number of silver coins to one side. "So you know I am in possession of the money I have promised, but so that you will not be paid before the reading. How's that? I believe that is fair."

Astre didn't like it. She had a feeling she knew how this was going to end, but she felt committed to do the reading now, and at least this way, she supposed, she might have a chance of keeping her fee *if* the fortune turned out to be in his favor.

"All right, then. You must pick how you would like your future to be revealed. You may choose from the tarot cards," she said, fanning the deck faced down out across the table. "Or we have the stones," she whispered, pulling a handful from the pouch to show the merchant a collection of river pebbles painted with symbols on their smooth surface. "Then there is the crystal ball." Astre pulled off the small square of cloth to reveal a crystal sphere bigger than the size of the merchant's fist. "And last, we have the tea leaves. You can choose your tea, which I shall brew in an age-old way and then you will need to drink it."

Silence filled the caravan as the merchant thought about the options before him. Eventually, Astre asked him, "So what shall it be?"

"Hmm...I do not like the sound of the tarot cards. I have heard ghastly tales about them so I won't pick those." Astre collected the cards back up and settled them in the wooden box that was sitting on the bed beside her. "As for tea, pah! I am a wine and ale man. Tea won't do." The cup and saucer were moved out of sight, leaving the crystal ball and stones for him to choose from. "The stones, I think. The stones...yes...they remind me of coins sitting in a money pouch, so that must be a good sign, eh?"

With that, Astre covered over the crystal ball once more and transferred it to a place of safety. Then she rounded up all the stones and returned them to the pouch, which she then handed to the merchant. "Close your eyes. Think of who you are. Think of the past, present and future. Now shake the pouch three times. Good," she said, nodding once it was done. Taking back possession of the little bag, she asked, "Are you ready to learn about your future? Be sure, for what you are about to hear is the truth. None, not you, not I, can stand in it's way. Once seen, it cannot be unseen. Once spoken, it cannot be unspoken."

"I am sure. Please, tell me what the stones say," he whispered in earnest, his eyes gleaming in the light of the lamp overhead.

Astre put her hand into the bag and pulled out three stones. She lay them in the center of the table. "This one represents lightning," she began.

"What does it mean?"

"Wait. We must read these three together, or not at all. This one," she said, pointing at the stone in the middle that had an arrow painted on it, "symbolizes direction. The last one carries the mark of prosperity."

"Prosperity - that's good. That's very good," the merchant grinned. "Please go on. Tell me about my fortune. Tell me about the fortune that is going to come to me."

Astre's brow furrowed. "Please, sir, you must not jump ahead nor twist my predictions to suit yourself."

"I don't understand. You said prosperity."

"That I did, though I did not say how it might figure - or not - in your destiny. As I have already explained, the stones must be read together. Now, listen to what they have to tell you..." Astre paused, arranging the words in the right order in her head. She was always careful with her words, for one slip of the tongue, one misunderstanding, could very well ruin her reputation.

"I am listening," the man said gravely. He did not like what the fortune teller had implied, and now he was worried.

"Misfortune is to be found on the road ahead," Astre warned the merchant. "You must be careful. The stones advise that you turn around."

"What? Turn around? Explain, madam." The man spoke gruffly.

"Sometimes the stones speak literally. What they say is exactly what they mean. At other times, they talk in riddles and to find the answer - or in this case, to learn of your fate - their words must be scrutinized for a hidden meaning."

"So which is it?"

"They are most certainly speaking literally. Perhaps there is something dangerous on this very road though I do not know what it could be. However, if you were to turn around and head back to the town, you could find a safer road to travel."

"I am not changing my plans because of some silly stones," the man scoffed.

"But," Astre pressed, "you might wish to reconsider surely if your prosperity was under threat." She used her finger to point at the final stone. "It would be best for you to find an alternative way, sir. It's what the stones counsel."

"This is preposterous! You said you would tell me my fortune, but all I have heard is some garbled, insubstantial threats and maybes. If you think I'm paying for this, you are mistaken, madam." Swiftly, he gathered up his coins and returned them to his money purse. Then he stormed out of the wagon, catching the tablecloth as he did so, causing all the stones to clatter to the floor. Astre gasped in shock and horror.

She exited the wagon to see the man climbing up onto his cart.

"You are a fake! A fraud!" he shouted, as he caught sight of her once more. "You cannot pull the wool over my eyes. I am no fool. You shall not have one penny from me. Not one!" He then turned his horse around and went off in the direction of the road.

Astre waited to see whether he would do as he had been told and head back towards the town or if he would ignore the warning he had been given. It was no surprise when he headed away from the settlement, but the fortune teller knew it was a decision he would come to regret. The merchant had upset the stones, and Astre knew that had consequences.

VI

The following day Astre decided it was time to move on. Her run-in with the merchant the previous day had tainted her enjoyment of a place that had seemed so perfect before his arrival.

After a light breakfast, she was on the road again. Astre, like the merchant, followed the road in the opposite direction of the town, but then she was all right to do so. She had not been warned against it.

The weather was warm and the sun shone as she made her way through the forest. Birdsong floated lazily on the air. Gradually, her mood lightened, if only a little.

However, mid-afternoon her countenance clouded as she rounded a bend to find that further along the road stood the familiar shape of the merchant. He was standing in the middle of the way while his cart waited forlornly, lopsided, at the side of the road.

Astre slowed down as she got nearer.

"Come to gloat, have you?" he snapped, angrily. "You horrible, wicked woman."

"What has happened here?" she asked, choosing to ignore his outburst.

"As if you don't know. You bewitched my horse. Don't deny it. I know it was you."

"I did no such thing. Now, please be sensible and tell me what has occurred."

"My horse became skittish and shied away from one side of the road, dragging the cart into the ditch on the other. The stupid beast has broken both wheels on that side. Both of them! Now, what am I going to do?"

"And the horse? How does it fair?" Astre wondered aloud as she climbed down to take a look. "Oh, you poor thing," she said, rubbing it's nose tenderly. "You've lamed your leg."

"Don't worry about that creature. Instead, help me to get my strong boxes off the back of the cart and into your wagon. Then you can take me to the next town, seeing as this is all your fault."

Again, Astre chose to ignore his comment, so full of concern was she for the horse. "But what of your horse, sir? It is hurt."

"If the horse is lame, madam, I shall have it disposed of and replaced. It is of no concern of yours," the man retorted, his lack of compassion obvious.

His tone when speaking of the horse upset Astre greatly, for she understood just how fine an animal her pony was and had a great respect and affection for it. It was for this very reason that she did what she did next. Keeping quiet so as not to alert the merchant, she untied the straps that tethered the horse to the cart. She might not be able to do much for it, but this much she could do. Then, very calmly, she walked back over to her wagon.

"My boxes are this way," the merchant barked.

"I will not be helping you with your boxes, sir," Astre replied flatly, climbing back up to her seat.

"Why ever not? You owe me this."

"I owe you nothing. You were warned that you would meet trouble on the road. You didn't listen."

"You did this to me! You! You cursed me. That's what you did. You cursed me."

"No, I did not. The blame lies entirely with you. You're the one who tried to cheat a fortune teller for your fortune. Perhaps next time you will think twice before being so dishonest." Astre turned away from the man, and with a click of her tongue, and a flick of the reins, her pony started to walk on. Out of the corner of her eye, she saw the merchant's horse begin to hobble away, back the way it had come, unbeknown to it's master.

On seeing that his only chance of rescue was leaving, he started to run but only managed a few paces before his great fashionable coat, made out of the heaviest and warmest wool, made the attempt impossible. Puffing, he called out, "Where are you going?" But Astre ignored him; he was not used to being ignored. "You cannot leave me here!" he protested angrily. "There are outlaws in the forest! I shall be robbed, my goods and possessions stolen!"

"'Tis a pity that you amassed so much, then, isn't it?" the fortune teller retorted, and with that, she moved beyond the hearing of his angry shouting.

It didn't take long for all thoughts of the bad-tempered merchant that had lingered with her since the first time she had spotted him at the market, to disappear from her mind. Striking up a song, she looked up at the bright sky as the caravan ambled along the forest road, onwards to the next town and the next market.

Rosina the Fortune Teller

E.W. Farnsworth

The handsomely dressed man sat down across the small table from Rosina, placed a fresh ten-dollar bill in the glass jar that sat by his elbow and extended his right hand, palm upwards. Rosina took the hand in her hands as if it were a precious book and gazed at it with focused intensity. With the index finger of her right hand, she traced the man's broken life line. She frowned a little, and she could feel the man's reaction to her expression in the way his hand pulled back slightly. She spoke.

"I see some big change in this line. I see loss of stability and loss of security. I see a problem in the direction in life." She fell silent to let her words sink in. Then she gently gave him back his hand and slid back in her wooden chair and looked him in the eye. His eyes were appreciative, asking for more. She shook her head a little and continued, "These things are in the past." She could tell that so far what she said was true because there was no change in his expression or in the dilation of the pupils of his eyes.

She asked her customer whether he wanted to have her read the cards. When the man nodded that, yes, he would like that very much, she drew from her embroidered skirts a tarot deck and placed four cards on the table, and the last of those was death. Rosina was disconcerted by the directness of the fortune. There was no ambiguity: the man clearly had a badly broken life line, and he was surely going to die. She thought his brown eyes were kind, and he seemed not to want to cause her discomfort through discovering his secret. Rosina wondered why, if he knew his fortune already, he had come to her today. She scanned his hand to be sure she had seen a wedding band, and she continued.

"You are a married man. Your wife does not know all that you know about your condition. You are afraid to tell her. You are afraid to admit it to yourself." He blinked, and his eyes welled up. He pursed his lips and then wet them with his tongue. "You did not want to know about your condition, but now you are afraid." The man nodded ever so slightly. *He is indeed afraid,* Rosina thought. She laid two more tarot cards on the table. "This card says that you are a fool, and that one says you are in league with dark forces."

"How can you possibly know these things?" the man asked her.

"You cannot escape from your destiny, yet you struggle. You think that by denying the truth, the truth will go away."

"So how do I deal with this so-called truth?"

"That is up to you. Death stands between you and your resolution. You must turn death to life. You know this, yet you waver."

"If my wife knew what I know, she would surely die of mortification. I cannot tell her."

"So you come to me to have what you know is true confirmed?"

"Yes, and to find a way to tell my wife."

"I can tell you what I see. I cannot tell you what to do."

"I see. But can you tell me what would happen to my wife if I told her?"

"I can only see what will be, not what may be."

"So tell me what you see. Here, I am putting another ten dollars in your jar. Please tell me."

"Relax. Close your eyes. Empty your mind of useless thoughts and images. Breathe in and out, in and out. Now take a deep breath and hold it. Now exhale. Again. And exhale. You have been troubled in your sleep. You have had nightmares. Tell me what you have seen."

"A creature with a rake comes at me. The creature will not leave me in peace. When I try to grasp it, I discover it is empty air."

"Can you see this creature now?"

"No."

"What do you see?"

"I see a troubled woman with dark eyes."

"Go on."

"The woman is striving to understand me."

"Yes?"

"Romnichels."

"I am Romnichels."

"I know." The man opened his eyes and gazed into Rosina's eyes with longing. Rosina knew the look well. She shook her head and blinked her eyes.

"So tell me why you are here—really."

"I had to see you."

"So now you see me."

"Yes."

"Sir that is all I can do for you today." Rosina rose from her chair and moved to the window. She drew the shade to let the noon light into the room. She looked out into the street crowded with people at lunch time. She heard the man's chair slide as he rose. She heard his footsteps as he walked to the door. She heard the door open, and then she heard it close. Rosina breathed out a sigh of relief. Then she turned around and looked at her little table with the jar and the tarot cards. She decided she would tidy up and have a smoke because in another fifteen minutes she had another appointment.

Rosina stacked her tarot cards and put them in the pocket of her dress. She took the two ten-dollar bills out of the glass jar, folded them and put them in her bodice between her breasts. She drew a scarf from a rack that stood back of her chair and tied it around her neck. Then she sat in her chair, pulled an ash tray out of a drawer on her side of the table, a box of Swan Vestas and a cigarette she had rolled for herself early that morning. She struck one Swan Vesta on the side of the box and lit her cigarette. She took a deep draught and held the smoke in her lungs before she breathed out. Smoke rose to the ceiling in a spiral pattern though the air in the room was still. Rosina watched the smoke as if it could tell her something, but it could not tell her a thing.

Rosina shrugged in resignation, grimaced and rose to close the blinds. Then she paced the room smoking her cigarette and thinking, only stopping to drop ash in her glass ashtray. *Do I have time to relieve myself before my next customer arrives? Probably not,* she thought. She told herself that she would just have to wait until afterward. She heard a knock on the door and put out her cigarette in the ashtray. She slid the ashtray and her Swan Vesta matchbox into the table drawer. She sat back in her chair, primped her raven-black hair, straightened her bright green scarf and said, "Enter!"

A pretty young woman entered and sat in the chair across from Rosina's. She put a five-dollar bill in the glass jar and held out her small right hand, palm upwards. After Rosina read the palm, she turned and fetched an Ouija board and changed the position of the chairs so that she and her customer could touch knees and face each other with the board between them on their laps. She placed her customer's fingers on her side of the small heart-shaped disc and told her to close her eyes. She placed her own fingers on the other side of the disc. She closed her eyes and waited. The disc moved, and then halted. Rosina opened her eyes. When she had examined the letter indicated by the pointer on the disc, she closed her eyes and the disc moved again. Rosina again opened her eyes to see the letter indicated by the disc. She repeated the operation five more times. When the disc refused to move further, Rosina told her customer that the session had ended and that she should open her eyes. Rosina restored the Ouija board with its disc and the two chairs to their original positions.

She opened her table drawer and extracted a blank piece of white stationery and a pencil. On the paper, she wrote the letters that had been identified in the Ouija session. She handed the paper to her customer, who burst into tears and crumpled the paper in her hand. Her customer sobbed uncontrollably, and Rosina allowed her to weep until she could weep no more. Rosina then handed the woman a colored handkerchief that she kept up her sleeve. The woman dried her eyes and blew her nose. Then she handed the handkerchief back to Rosina. Without a word, she stood and uncertainly made her way to the door through which she had entered the room and went out into the street.

When Rosina thought her customer had left the vicinity, she put the handkerchief in a bundle of laundry, retrieved the five-dollar bill from the glass jar on the table and folded it before she put it between her breasts. She threw open the drapery that covered the window and checked the clock for the time. Satisfied that she had done a good morning's work, Rosina threw on a shawl, closed up her shop and went to her mother's apartment to prepare her lunch.

Rosina's mother, Hola, was of the old school. She, her husband and children had come from England over forty years ago and somehow managed to keep body and soul together by telling fortunes and keeping animals. They had arrived in America bringing a dog and a bear, both of which could do tricks. Rosina's father had been a workhorse buyer for those rich enough to have the money to buy them. He also cared for the animals for a weekly fee. Rosina's mother had told fortunes for the rich and famous of her day. She never talked about her secrets with her daughter because she believed that each generation had to make it on its own merits. This was a family tradition extending back as far as human memory. Hola said that some gifts passed from mother to daughter in the bloodline and that her family's origins traced back to the Egyptians. Around her neck Hola wore a small metal ankh as a token of this fact, and she told her daughter that when she died, that ankh would pass to her.

Hola's health was not good these days and she could not walk long distances. So Rosina shopped for her mother and checked on her in the morning, in the late afternoon and in the evening. Rosina's sisters and brothers had migrated from New York when they were old enough to break out on their own. They had never bothered to tell their parents or Rosina where they were going or what they intended to do. Hola would talk about Rosina's siblings, but Rosina knew that her mother's dreams for her children did not account for the realities of the harsh American life. Romani's were not discriminated against in America as they were in England and on the Continent of Europe, but connections helped in this land of opportunity, and Romani's only had other Romani's to help them. The grass was deemed by all Romani's to be greener everywhere but where they resided, and that vision kept them moving all over the world. That was fine when they stayed together in large bands of many families. Their fabric of life broke up when they set out on their own.

When she pushed open the door of her mother's apartment, Rosina knew that she had her work cut out for her that day. She flung open all the window shades to let light into the house, and she called out to her mother to discover what room she occupied today. From the bedroom, Hola hollered a greeting and asked that Rosina come to help her get to the living room. Rosina found her mother fully clothed in a comfortable chair across from her bed. The bed was properly made and had clippings and photographs littered all over the spread.

"Look there at your father smiling next to that bear. Hugo was the bear's name, and he had an appetite!"

"Yes, Mama, I know about Hugo and how you brought him over from England and how he made all sorts of money for you when you first arrived. Let's get to the living room so I can make you some herbal tea."

When Hola had walked down the hall and sat in her chair in the living room, Rosina brought her tea and tidied up the place while she talked.

"I had two customers today. One married man whose only purpose was to try to bed me. One unmarried woman, probably pregnant by a man named Charles, who wept bitterly when his name was revealed by the Ouija. Here, I brought you the extra ten dollars that the man gave me for my trouble." Rosina drew out the cash she had sequestered in her bosom and gave one of the ten-dollar bills to her mother, who folded it up and put it between her breasts in the family tradition.

"Why don't you find a man to take care of you? You have beauty and youth now, but you won't have them for much longer, believe me. Maybe this customer who sees you wants to divorce his wife and marry you!"

"Mama, I can tell when a man wants me for my body. That man will never leave his wife because he is a coward at heart. Besides, he does not have the gypsy fire in his blood. I would eat him alive and drain his feeble spirit. I would rather live alone. And then there's you. How could I continue to help you if I were a drudge in my own home, especially if I had children?"

"Rosina, you must have children. I had eight children by your father, and they made my life complete."

"Perhaps, but they are all gone—who knows where?—and I'm the one that's left."

"You have to bear children when you are young."

"You had me when you were over forty years old."

"Yes, I did, and it almost killed me to have you. The doctor told me you had to be my last." For a long time after that, the mother and daughter were silent while Rosina dusted the room. Then she went into the kitchen and cleaned the dishes, and finally, she filled a bucket and washed her mother's soiled linens. She rinsed them in the sink, wrung them out by hand and hung them on a line out the back window with clothespins. Then she returned to the living room to help her mother put her feet up on a small chair and then covered her mother with a shawl that she had crocheted herself.

"Thank you, Rosina. I remember when you crocheted this shawl. Oh, I forgot. A young man dropped by early this morning just after you left. He left a letter addressed to you. I was good—I did not read the letter. I do not recognize the handwriting, but I know it was not a woman's hand that wrote it." Hola pointed to her roll-top desk in the corner. Rosina rolled up the top and saw on top of piles of letters and newspapers a thick letter with her name and her mother's address. The cancelation was done in Chicago. Rather than read it right away, Rosina put the letter in the pocket of her dress. She then closed the desk, did a few more chores, kissed her now sleeping mother goodbye and went home to her own apartment.

Rosina did not immediately read the letter when she arrived at her apartment. She busied herself doing her own chores. She had some tea with crackers. She touched up a drawing that lay on her easel. She dusted. Finally, she realized she was just putting off the inevitable, so she opened the letter and read it. Of course, it was from Robert begging her to drop everything and take the next train to Chicago. He said he missed her and wanted her with him always. He pled with her and told her how much she meant to him. He wrote that he was having great success and that he knew she would love the Windy City as much as he did. He said he would telegraph her the money to travel as soon as she agreed to come. She set her lips in a line and sat down at her kitchen table. There in a rack were all Robert's other letters from the time he had left after high school. She had kept them all, though from time to time she wanted to burn them in the grate and be done with them and Robert forever. Among the letters were his pictures. Robert by the lake. Robert by the opera house. Robert in the park. Robert with a male friend. Robert looking as if he was full of himself. Robert looking abysmally sad. She had her own pictures of Robert. Robert and Rosina at the high school prom. Robert and Rosina next to a canoe. Robert and Rosina at Coney Island. Robert and Rosina feeding swans.

Rosina recalled the last time she had told Robert's fortune. She had managed to remain calm through it all, but it had broken her heart. She saw that he had to leave New York and never return. She saw that he had to find his own way in life in a new city far away. She saw that he had to remain single because for a long while he could not afford to marry. She had seen his life so clearly then, but there was no place for a Romani in it. She was almost frantic looking for some sign that she would be tucked somewhere in the life she envisioned for Robert, but she was nowhere to be found in it. When she told Robert his fortune, she could see in his eyes that he liked everything she told him about himself. She also knew that he understood nothing of what she was feeling about having to tell him his fortune. He did not ask about where she fit into the picture. It was probably just as well, she thought. She might have broken down and cried when she told him the truth—that she could see no way for her to fit in.

So Robert had departed, and every month or two he sent Rosina a letter. Initially, the letters were those of a lonely man in a crowded, foreign city. Robert was a poet in those letters, and her heart rose when she read his words because they were so evocative and personal. Then Robert got traction in Chicago and made friends. Now his letters were catalogs of things and people he had seen. His writing style was more detached. At times, his impressions seemed forced as if he had not taken the time to digest what he wrote about but out of duty jotted down his thoughts to fill the pages. When Robert landed the job that worked for him, he wrote a very long letter that alluded to the future they had dreamed of when they were in high school before their dreams were shattered by his leaving. For many letters after that, he was focused on the challenges of his job and his relations with his co-workers. Robert was studying so much to become an expert in his profession, he had little time to write much more than a postcard. Ironically, the more pictures he sent, the less his letters really said. It seemed to her that she had become for him more of a listening post and less of a person.

Lately, though Robert had reverted to the man she knew and loved in those lonely letters of his early time in Chicago. Gradually his poetry crept back, and the cadence of his prose was like himself, only more so. Rosina did not know what had happened to change him, and she feared looking into the matter because she was afraid it was love of someone else. She did, however, begin to enjoy his letters again and to look forward to receiving them. As for her responses to his letters, she had always sent her letters by return post. She had never presumed to write out of cycle for many reasons. The major reason was that she never knew when he might write his final letter having found another woman. Nothing exasperated her more than imagining Robert and some significant other reading her letter together. Then again, because Robert had never been explicit in his letters, Rosina never had a sense of his commitment to her except as an epistolary companion.

Rosina reviewed the reasons things had not worked out with Robert. Her family had not approved of her marrying someone who was not Romani. They said—particularly her mother had said—that no outsider could possibly understand the gypsy soul. Hola had repeatedly said that Robert was a nice boy, but he did not have the soul of a Romnichel. Rosina watched as her brothers and sisters went their own ways, many of them marrying people who were not Romnichels, but the rules for Romani seemed only to apply to her and to none of her siblings. She was the heir to her mother's sixth sense. She had the fiery Romani eyes and razor sharp wit. She dressed like a Romani, and she had the almost masculine talent for excision and exclusion that complemented her willfulness and ingenuity. She knew how to be loyal and to hold onto a good idea against all opposition. Why, then, she asked herself, did she not telegraph Robert that she loved him, she had always loved him, and she wanted to come to him immediately to be his bride? She hesitated to do that because she thought he should first be explicit about their relationship and because she had to think of caring for her mother.

So Rosina laid Robert's latest letter on her kitchen table and sorted through her stationary drawer to find what she needed to compose a reply. She decided it was time for her to call the question. Robert needed to know that she required a proposal. Nothing less would do. If he wanted to discuss things, perhaps he should come to New York by train and talk. Rosina was of two minds writing this letter because she both loved one dimension of Robert as she remembered him and because she hated the idea of being taken for granted by him. She needed to know the score. If Robert was unwilling or unable to make a commitment, then perhaps they should stop corresponding. She had never felt as conflicted or sad since she read Robert's fortune and catalyzed all her pain from his departure.

When she had completed her letter, Rosina sat at her table for a long time brooding. She daydreamed until it was dark outside and she heard the night sounds of the city below her apartment. She looked at the clock to discover that she had just enough time to reach her mother's apartment to help her get ready for bed in the usual way.

Rosina tucked her mother in, and Hola looked at her daughter appraisingly. She knew something was wrong, and her eyes asked what it was. The daughter could hide nothing from her mother because of what they were. They shared the sixth sense, after all. So Rosina told her mother about the latest letter from Robert and the letter she had just written in response. Her mother listened without interrupting. Then she spoke softly in a way and with words that Rosina had not expected.

"Take another look into Robert's fortune. Find yourself there. Then do what you must. Do not think of me. Do not think of anything else but you and Robert. If you are in his future, that is all that matters." Rosina almost wept for joy, but she knew her mother's wiles and she knew the power of fortunes. She had read Robert's fortune before, and that fortune contained nothing about her at all. What if she read it again and came up with the same result? She wondered whether she could bear that savage truth.

So for a week, Rosina continued doing what she did without resorting to consulting Robert's fortune. She read palms, conducted séances with the dead, worked the Ouija board, drew tarot cards, constructed horoscopes and all the other fortune teller tasks—for paying customers. She made a lot of money and many of her customers scheduled appointments for her to fit in her crowded agenda. She was clearly still very much in demand. People were desperate to know the future, and nothing could substitute for a genuine fortune teller to give them what they wanted. Convinced that she had created a clientele and a lasting career, Rosina felt independent and free. She wondered how consulting Robert's fortune could change that. She had changed since high school, and so had Robert. However the fortune turned out, would they be compatible? Would they share the kind of love now that they had once shared in their youth? How would their feelings for each other translate into a family with children?

Ironically, the event that stimulated Rosina to act was another encounter with the disturbed married man who wanted to bed her. This encounter turned into a shouting match where he accused Rosina of knowing full well how he felt about her and she accused him of seeing her under false pretenses. The man did not raise his hand to strike her, but he looked her in the eye with violence and told her that he could not do without her anymore. He demanded that she discover that he and his wife would separate and that she would become his wife. Rosina was outraged by this intrusion on her fortune telling integrity, and she told the man to leave her establishment and never come to her again. She ushered him to her door and when he exited, she slammed it behind him. Then she broke down and cried in frustration and rage. She felt very lucky that the man had not raped her.

That afternoon Rosina told her mother about the incident and what she had done. Hola only nodded and smiled as if she had been through similar trials. She saw beyond the incident to what was really bothering Rosina, and she suggested to her daughter that it was time to look into Robert's fortune. She said that some men and women were so taken by the intimacy of fortune telling that they confused the professional intimacy with physical intimacy. In fact, she said, those who performed reader and advisor services who were not Romani often performed prostitution as part of their business. Hola said those were pretenders to both trades. She advised her daughter to examine her feelings and motives carefully because once she embarked on the path she had chosen, she could not turn back.

So Rosina assembled all of Robert's letters at her kitchen table and she lit a red candle. She pulled out each of the pictures he had sent and examined them carefully in the order they had arrived. She did not reread the man's letters for she remembered every word in all of them. When she felt ready, she looked into the flame dancing on the top of the candle wick and envisioned. Rosina knew how to clear her thoughts of everything that might distract her, and she was soon in a self-induced trance that was enhanced by the flame. Robert was suddenly there, and he was alone by a lake. He had a bag of crumbs, and he was feeding water birds the crumbs. He looked up as if he had heard something and turned to look directly at her. He smiled as he had done characteristically when they were an acknowledged couple in high school. Rosina knew that he was looking directly at her and at no one else. She could not see herself in the vision because the vision was looking at her. When she came out of her trance,

Rosina shuddered to think of the meaning of this epiphany. Could she have mistaken the fortune she had read for Robert after high school? Could she have failed to see herself in his life because she was so integrally part of him that she could not be a separate figure in it? She was confused by her thoughts. She hyperventilated because she felt she needed air. She went for a long night walk in the city streets to consider what she had learned.

The next day Rosina had two experiences that shook her, both of which were reported in the New York newspapers. First, the unmarried woman who had come to her and got the name Charles from the Ouija board committed suicide by jumping off the Brooklyn Bridge. Her body was fished from the river, and the coroner proclaimed that she had been pregnant at the time of her drowning. Second, the man who had violently shouted at her and, she thought, had designs on her body, was found murdered in his home by his insanely jealous wife. In confessing to the crime, the woman said she thought her husband was sleeping with a gypsy who was a prostitute and paying her a lot of money for his pleasure. She had confronted him, and her husband confessed that he loved his fortune teller madly and wanted a divorce so he could marry her. According to the news reports, she shot him between the eyes with his own pistol and then calmly called the police to report the fact.

Rosina read the headlines with shock and the stories with increasing horror. In both instances, she had played an unwitting but critical role. Her cooperation with the Ouija board had elicited the name Charles and confirmed for the troubled woman what she already suspected. Her being accosted by the married man led him in frustration to tell his wife a lie and ask for a divorce at the worst possible time, psychologically speaking. Rosina had not been named in any of the press coverage, so she thought she was probably safe from intrusion on her privacy by investigative reporters. She knew, however, that the wife of the married man might just as easily have tried to kill her as her husband. She had a frisson of fear that one of the woman's relatives might try to find out who the vaunted fortune teller was and eliminate her for the sake of family honor. That was the way her Romani mind worked in this instance.

The convergence of events, however, summed up to her need to sort out quickly how Robert felt about her and to get her life realigned purposefully. Two days after the headlines hit the papers, Hola received another letter from Robert answering Rosalina's letter that called the question. She did not read the letter in Hola's presence but, as she always did, took Robert's precious correspondence to her apartment and, in a calm attitude, opened and read it.

Robert was now clear in every way Rosina could have wished. He professed that she was the only woman he had ever loved. He stated that he wanted to marry her at the earliest opportunity and to be with her always after that. He volunteered to pay her way to Chicago to hear all this from himself, or he would come to New York on the next available train to get on his knees and ask her to marry him. He also wrote that if her mother was in need of her attention, he would be happy to find an apartment for her in Chicago and pay for her travel and settlement there. He said that he knew of a place not far from his own apartment where the travel between apartments would not be onerous for Rosina. He enclosed a very recent picture of himself to give her an indication of how he looked at present, and from her perspective, he was a sight for her sore eyes. Between the letter and the picture, she had everything she thought she wanted. When that evening she went to see Hola, she laid out what Robert had said and what she felt about it. She did not do this excitedly because she wanted her mother to know that hers was not an infatuation but a conviction. When Hola heard what her daughter had to say, a tear rolled down her cheek, and she opened her arms to enfold her daughter. She said she was the happiest person on earth, and she began babbling about how interesting it would be to discover Chicago. It would be the beginning of a whole new life for both of them. She did not say one thing that implied objection, and Rosina thought at the time that all her doubts and fears had been dispelled in a single afternoon. She left her mother sleeping peacefully and returned to her apartment and after she reread Robert's letter four times to be sure of what it implied, to compose her reply.

Rosina wrote carefully, crafting her words for precision but making each phrase positive. She wrote that she felt exactly as Robert said he did. She had never loved any other man, and his proposal was the key that unlocked their combined futures. She wrote that she did not care whether she went to Chicago or Robert came to New York, they had to meet face to face to talk and enjoy each other's company. She thanked him for enclosing his picture—he appeared just as she had imagined he would. She enclosed the most recent picture of herself so that he would not be surprised by her current appearance. She signed her letter, "All My Love, Rosina," just as she had signed the picture in his copy of their high school yearbook. She sealed the letter and put a stamp on it. In the morning on the way to her office room, she mailed the letter and expected that it would be in Chicago within the next four days, perhaps five at the most. She thought that he would most probably send a telegram with instructions or even show up at the train station and call Hola's home telephone from there.

In the meantime, Rosina continued with her fortune-telling business and with taking care of her mother. She seemed to be able to do much more than she ever had done before and with significantly less effort. She ascribed her facility to having a great weight of doubt and worry taken from her shoulders. She suddenly felt ten years younger. She thought she might actually be happy. The euphoria she felt had only one drawback and it was unintended and wholly unlooked for: her sixth sense was no longer at its peak of perfection. She had trouble focusing on her customers' needs. She was so preoccupied with the prospect of being with Robert again that her hopes and dreams interfered with her business. Her customers did not notice that this was happening, but Rosina knew it was so. Even when her prescience was spot on, she had doubts about it. She had never doubted her gifts before, and this worried her.

Rosina asked her mother how her powers as a fortune teller were affected by her relationship with her husband. Hola spent a while considering what her daughter was really asking. She said that she and her husband had grown into love rather than fallen in love. That way, she said, her powers were never affected by their relationship. They were so very busy relocating and getting settled in a new country and so worried about every nickel that they earned, they had no time to become infatuated. Hola asked Rosina why she had asked the question. Rosina told her mother that she felt her powers had been affected by her love for Robert. She said she was wildly happy as she had been only in her last year of high school before telling Robert's fortune drove them apart until just recently. Hola nodded reflectively, and she told her daughter that loving Robert evidently did not affect her vision after high school, but Rosina said that perhaps it had done so. She explained what she had learned from envisioning him in the flame. Perhaps, she said, her lover's fortune had been a false apprehension. With tears in her eyes, she said she might have erred by not conceiving that she was to be with him even though she could not see herself in the vision with him.

Hola now understood her daughter well. She told Rosina that she had once made the same mistake with a prospective lover when she was being courted by her father and many other men. The man was the dashing son of the leader of one of the most powerful Romani families. He probably would have become her children's father except that he asked Hola to tell his fortune. Unable to see herself in his life, she told him that he would depart from his family and establish a new dynasty outside it. He had done so and with a girl who was not a Romani, he had sired thirteen children. The man never forgot Hola's fortune because he attributed to it all of his successes, including wealth, a large family, and good health. Meanwhile, Hola said, she had suffered in despair for weeks when she saw how her fortune played out in the young man's life. She ached because she could not experience with him the joys he felt with another woman. Hola was changed by his success. She said she never could love another man as she had that scion whose fortune she had created. She finished her rhapsody and fell silent while mother and daughter considered the implications of what she had said.

"So this is the destructive power of our fortune telling. You told what you thought was the truth and it changed your life forever. I told what I thought was the truth and the same thing happened to me. The only difference was that you married my father and had children and I married no one and remained available."

"Yes, but I grew to love your father. And I loved you children, every one. I can speculate what might have been with the other man, but I'll never know for sure what would have been better than what I received. I was so very lucky in ways I never could have conceived of before I experienced your father and you children."

"I have lost so many years to the illusion I created for Robert, and so has he. We might have been together all the time. How can we make up for what we have lost?"

"Lost? Rosina, just think of what you've gained!" Rosina saw that her mother needed sleep, so she waited quietly while Hola calmed down and closed her eyes. She turned out her light and locked and left the apartment. She returned to her own apartment and went to bed. She tossed and turned all night thinking about Robert and what might have been. In the morning she was tired, but she had also become resigned to looking forward, not backward. She decided that she would not worry about the years that she and Robert had missed. She looked forward to hearing from him and having the details of their reunion spelled out in clear terms.

Rosina waited for ten days, but she heard nothing from Robert. She began asking every day whether Hola had received a letter addressed to her, but she said she had not received any letters at all. After fourteen days without a reply from him, Rosina wrote another letter to Robert. This letter was unique in all the years of their correspondence because she had never written him twice successively. She had always waited for his latest letter before she replied. In this case, she had made an exception because of the importance of the issues they had discussed. How could Robert have delayed in responding to her last letter? Had her picture upset him? Was he having second thoughts about proposing? Was he having trouble at work? She had another thought: perhaps Robert was sick or even dead. She realized that she had no way of knowing what his condition was. She had his address, but she had no telephone number for him. She tried to discover his number through his address but was informed by the operator that his number was unlisted. Rosina decided she would mail her second letter, and if she did not receive a response in another fortnight after that, she would scrape together the money to go to Chicago on her own to talk with him.

Rosina was so worried about Robert that she lost sleep and failed to eat and drink properly. She became pale and sickly. She checked with Hola every time they met about any contact that might have come from Robert by any means, but none came. At the end of the fortnight, having heard nothing more from Robert for almost a month, Rosina decided to take the train to Chicago and go to his door to see him. She was able to make the payment for the train passage, but she had very little left over after she made it. She took two apples and a sandwich with her so that she would not have to buy food, and she slept in the open carriage for the journey. When she arrived in Chicago, she was bewildered by the novelty of the place. She asked directions to Robert's address. Because she could not afford a taxicab, she walked the long distance. She finally found his door and knocked on it, but he was not at home. She sat down on the floor outside his door and waited. Romani's are very good at waiting, she thought. She remembered her mother's stories about waiting in lines to get passage and waiting in lines to get an apartment and waiting in lines to birth her children at hospitals that were reluctant to admit Romani's.

All through the night, Rosina waited, but Robert did not come. The next day Rosina was hungry, but she was reluctant to spend money, so she made her way to the bus station and used the restroom facilities there. She sat on the floor in the main terminal and told the passersby that she would tell their fortune for a quarter. Several people stopped to have their fortunes read, so by noon she had enough to buy a coffee, a donut, and an apple. She then returned to Robert's apartment to camp out on his doorstep. When by evening he had not returned, she tried to find the apartment manager, and she told him she was looking for her friend Robert who lived in Apartment 403. The manager verified that the man named Robert lived in that apartment, but he had no idea where Robert was. In fact, he had not seen Robert in almost a month. He remembered the last day he saw him because on that day Robert had paid his month's rent in cash and informed him that he might be gone for a while, but he would return.

When Rosina asked the apartment manager for a pencil and piece of paper, he gave them to her with a courtesy she had never known anyone exhibit in New York. She wrote a brief note to Robert that she had come to Chicago to find him, but he was clearly out of town. She wrote that she would be returning to New York as soon as she scraped together the money to make the trip. She wrote that she would be in the train station telling fortunes until she returned to New York. Finally, she wrote that she loved him and hoped that he was all right. She begged him to write her care of her mother as he always had done so that she would know he was all right.

Rosina was now very worried about Robert. She told fortunes at the railroad station and used the station's facilities for basic hygiene. In brief, she became the typical gypsy fortune teller living by her wits.

At least once a day she was propositioned as if she were a common prostitute and she indignantly refused the requests. She was so insightful in her fortunes that she enjoyed lines of customers. She doubled her rates, and the lines continued. She doubled her rates again, yet the people lined up to hear her read their palms. She was hassled by police daily, but the gentlemen who patronized her business quietly dissuaded the authorities from enforcing their vagrancy ordinance.

One young man, a graduate student at the university, asked Rosina whether she wanted to shift her location to the university where students needed to know their fortunes prior to exams and prior to interviewing for jobs. He was persuasive, and she intuitively felt that he was not going to abuse her. She moved into the student's apartment temporarily and set up shop in the university commons area. There she became a kind of overnight institution. Students flocked to have their fortunes told. Junior professors came to her about their prospects for tenure. Female students sought her advice about suitors and their future.

Within three weeks Rosina had made enough money to pay her passage back to New York. She thanked her benefactor for allowing her to stay in his apartment, for her encouragement in her hour of need, for the many meals and drinks he had bought for her and, most of all, for letting her use his bathroom and soap and shampoo. She gave the man, whose name was Rinaldo, her mother's address if he should ever come to New York, and he walked her to the station to see her off.

Rosina arrived back in New York and discovered that her mother had managed to get along without her daily ministrations. Hola was well and concerned about her daughter's health. She complimented Rosina on her resourcefulness while she was in Chicago. About Robert, she did not know what to say because still no mail or other word had come from him. Rosina's clients had left notes under her business door with wishes for her speedy return or recovery or both. Some of the notes reminded her of how much her clients needed her and how much they missed their contact with her. Even after her prolonged absence, she managed to pick right up with her business and to bargain with her landlord for late payment of her rent. Within two weeks Rosina was back up to par with her business appointments and she had paid her back rent in full. Robert now seemed to her like a phantom of the past with little relation to her life. She felt a fool for having gone to Chicago looking for him, but she felt stronger for having survived the trip and used her wits to make money the hard, gypsy way.

Robert never did communicate with Rosina again. She never knew what happened to him. She never wished him harm. In fact, she hoped sincerely that he was well and happy. Nevertheless, she took an irrevocable step and burned all Robert's correspondence and pictures in her fire grate. She thus turned a page in her life. Now resigned to her lot as a Romani fortune teller eking out a life in New York and tending to the needs of her mother Hola, Rosina once again became confident in her trade. Because she had no distractions, she had no trouble engaging her sixth sense. Her clients raved about the results of their encounters with her. She thought she had achieved equilibrium in her life and work, but something deep inside her told her that she had other adventures ahead. A still small voice kept telling her to keep an open mind and go with the flow of things as they came.

Two years after Rosina returned from Chicago, she was tidying her business room to prepare for a client in the early afternoon. She hoped to make the encounter with her client brief because the woman was an unutterable bore who wanted to drone on about a man who paid her no attention. She answered a knock on her door, and there stood Rinaldo looking sheepish.

"Hello, Rosina. Your mother told me where you worked. I was in the city and thought I would just drop by."

"Hi, Rinaldo. This is so unexpected. I have a client coming but come right in. It is good to see you again. I am eternally grateful for what you did for me in Chicago."

"It was the best I could do at the time, and I'd do it again, gladly. You are sure looking well. I don't want to intrude, but maybe after you've finished your business for the day, we could have dinner somewhere and catch up. I'd enjoy your company."

"Rinaldo, I don't know what to say. My mother usually counts on me.

"She told me. You visit her in the late afternoon, and then you return to tuck her into bed. That gives us just enough time for dinner in between if you're not too exhausted. We both have to eat, and I'm planning to pay—with no strings attached. Your mother knows the plan, and she said she'd like me to come back with you when you go to tuck her in."

"So, Rinaldo, did my mother have anything to do with your being in New York City?"

"It was you who gave me your mother's address before you left Chicago. You said I should make contact with you through her if I ever needed to. I did need to, so I looked her up and we had a chance to become acquainted. I never told you that I am half-Romani, did I? Well Hola saw immediately that I had gypsy blood, and that explained for her why I took you in. Your mother has quite an eye. I'm also impressed by her wit."

"Hola's wit? You must be kidding."

"She said you went looking for a man in Chicago and came home thinking you hadn't found him, but you had. You just didn't know it at the time."

"Hahaha. I must have a talk with my mother."

"We'll talk with her together after dinner. What do you say? I'll meet you at her place in the late afternoon, we'll get dinner and when we return, we'll all just talk. Is that all right with you?"

"I don't know."

"Please say you'll come. I came to see you again because I missed you. I earned my degree. So all my studying paid off nicely. I've a job and a new apartment in Chicago, but I'm to travel here once a month. I'm here on business that must be done tomorrow, so I'm free today and tonight. Please come to dinner with me. Wait, why don't we all three go to dinner. We'll invite Hola to go with us. Now you're smiling."

"If Hola will come with us, then that will be fine. So I'll see you at her place around five o'clock. Remember that we have to get her back by nine. She gets very tired, and her schedule must remain regular." Then Rosina told Rinaldo that he had to let her finish preparing for her customer and she shooed him out the door. When he had left, she was disconcerted and distracted. It took her five minutes to collect her wits. When her customer arrived, she was all business on the surface and all excitement on the inside. Rinaldo had meant nothing to her but a convenience in Chicago. She had been impressed by the sensitivity in his eyes, but he was always intent on his studies and never paid her any attention, or so she thought.

Rinaldo arrived as he had promised at Hola's, and both Rosina and Hola were dressed for dinner in the gypsy way. Rinaldo waved down a taxi, which drove them to an excellent restaurant that the women would never have afforded as a matter of thrift. When they had been seated, Rinaldo made it clear that the meal was his treat and he ordered a bottle of good red wine to breathe as they looked over the menu. When the waiter had taken their orders, Rinaldo launched into his life on the road as a Romani circus performer. He told stories of wandering throughout America with the jugglers, weight lifters, animal handlers and trapeze artists. His real father had been a wealthy industrialist who fell in love with his gypsy mother and sired Rinaldo but was unfortunately already married to a rich debutante. So he had given Rinaldo's mother money and she had raised him all by herself until she married the circus strong man Ruggiero. With the strong man, she had birthed eight other children, Rinaldo's siblings. When Rinaldo turned twelve, his real father returned to the circus when it came back to his town, and he bargained with the gypsy to allow him to educate his bastard son. So Rinaldo went to a fine set of private schools, then college preparatory school and finally college and graduate school. The circus boy became a doctor with a robe and a cap. Now he was called a success. Rinaldo smiled and winked when he said he could still calm a bear and make her dance.

Hola was delighted by everything Rinaldo said, but when he mentioned the bear, she laughed out loud and told stories about Hugo the bear that she and her husband had brought to America from England. She asked Rinaldo how his large family was doing today. At this Rinaldo became serious because the family had just been through a difficult time. It had nothing to do with money because Romani's had no trouble finding ways to get by. It had to do with Ruggiero and a circus master who had raped his sister. He did not go into the grisly details of the crime, but he said that the circus master was found dead with an iron bar twisted around his neck. At this news, Hola proposed a toast to gypsy justice. Rosina watched as her mother revealed Romani mannerisms she had not seen since she was a little girl. Rinaldo was clearly a hit with Hola, and Rosina finally admitted that she liked Rinaldo too. He was manly, witty, a great story teller, handsome and suave. He was a Romani, to be sure, but he was a gentleman as well. Rosina understood why the man had responded to her in her need. He did that because she was one of his people, and he felt he owed her hospitality.

Near the end of the dinner, Rinaldo told the two women that he almost regretted not having remained with the circus where you knew the people you worked with and you shared the hardships of gypsy life on the road. He said in his current business, he had to mistrust all his colleagues because they would knife him in the back for no reason at all. He was going to be on the road as a part of his job. He was based in Chicago, and there he kept his apartment. At least one week a month he would be staying in a hotel in New York, so he hoped to see Hola and Rosina at least once for dinner while he was in town. The women seemed delighted at the prospect. Full and happy after their dinner, the three returned to Hola's apartment and Rosina tucked her mother in. After that, Rinaldo wanted to escort Rosina home, and she allowed him to do that. When he said goodbye outside her door, he looked into her eyes with such burning sincerity that Rosina finally looked away blushing. Rinaldo promised her that he would woo and win and marry her, but not all in one night. Then he kissed Rosina's hand, walked down the steps to her apartment and vanished into the night.

Rosina felt giddy and confused by the whole encounter. Reflecting on the day and the dinner, she decided she was grateful for all that Rinaldo had done. She knew that her mother would be ecstatic with the possibility that Rinaldo was the perfect match for her. Instinctively she knew that Rinaldo might be just that—her perfect match, but she did not want to get her hopes up only to be let down as she had been with Robert. She mused that one week each month would allow a relationship to blossom—or not. As she drifted off to sleep, she had a vision of herself and Rinaldo surrounded by children and circus animals. In the vision, Rinaldo introduced Rosina to a huge female bear, and it danced for her just as Hola had danced for Rosina's father when he asked her to show the children how Hugo used to dance when they first came to America.

Rosina and Rinaldo

E.W. Farnsworth

Rosina and Rinaldo stopped by the duck pond in Central Park to feed the waterfowl. It was their third such outing in three days, and Rosina was feeling comfortable in Rinaldo's company. He was tall, well built, handsome and intelligent. He was also a good storyteller, particularly when he spun his tales about working in a traveling circus in his youth. Rinaldo was quiet now and looked serious as he littered the surface of the water with crumbs from his bag of stale bread. Rosina also scattered crumbs on the water from her bag. Ducks and geese swam towards them anticipating a feast, and the pair did not deny them their pleasure. They selectively threw the bread so that each bird had a chance to feast.

"Tell me again why you came to New York, Rinaldo." She was looking out over the water, waiting for a pair of mallard ducks to get close enough to feed.

"I came here for business, and I came for you. I just had to see you again. You gave me your mother's address, remember?"

"I do remember. You were so kind to put me up in Chicago. I don't know what I would have done if you hadn't come to my rescue."

"From the moment I saw you, I knew you were a survivor. The way you set up shop wherever you were to tell your fortunes brought back memories from my childhood. The world can be cruel, but we gypsies manage to make do, don't we?"

"Did Hola remind you why I was in Chicago in the first place?" Rosina was looking at him expectantly now, squinting because the day was so bright.

"Your mother told me that you were chasing an old flame that somehow disappeared. I told her that you found a new flame in me though you did not know it at the time. You weren't looking for me, but there I was. And here I am now in Central Park feeding the birds with you." He smiled at her and shrugged. Then he reached into his bag and brought out a few large pieces of bread. He hesitated for a moment. Then he threw the bread to a family of waiting ducks and ducklings, who fought over the bread pieces nearest them. "We've been through all these matters several times. Why are you still curious?"

"I just find it unbelievable that things worked out so...unexpectedly." She threw bread in the direction of the geese that swam out beyond the ducks. "As a professional fortune teller, I'm supposed to know the future, but I surely missed something important this time."

"You mean me?"

"Yes, I mean you, silly."

"I'm flattered to discover that I'm important to you. Is that the way you really feel about me now?"

"At first, I was surprised. Now that we've been together I'm getting used to your being here, but tomorrow morning you're going to go back to Chicago again. It's such a long way. I don't know what I will do when you're gone. I'll miss you."

"I'm sorry I have to go. It's business. You know that. I've also told you and Hola that I'll be back again soon. Have you and she given any more thought about moving to Chicago permanently?"

"My last venture to Chicago ended so badly."

"It didn't end badly from my perspective. Your visit changed my life for the better. I couldn't get you out of my mind. In fact, I can't get you out of my mind even when you're here beside me." He arced a large piece of bread far out on the pond. Waterfowl raced out to claim the prize.

"It took you a while to be in touch after I left Chicago. Two whole years you waited!"

"You grew on me slowly. I had to finish graduate school and get a job. Only when I was ready to be serious, I came. I'm lucky you are still single."

"I had almost resigned myself to being a spinster." She turned to see his reaction to this thought.

"Rosina, that would be a terrible thing. I find you irresistible. I must be with you. The thought of being away eats at my heart. I brought you something to remember me by while I'm in Chicago."

"You did? What did you bring me?" Rosina was excited by the prospect of a keepsake.

"It's right in my pocket." Rinaldo reached in his coat pocket and withdrew a small jewelry box. "Here." He handed the box to her.

"Here, let me hold your bag of bread while you open it."

She looked at the box in her hand and then looked up at him. She handed him her bag and prized the box open.

"It's a beautiful ring. Oh, Rinaldo, it's so wonderful. It sparkles like a diamond."

"That's because it is a diamond. I hope the ring fits you. Hola gave me your ring size. Please put it on." She slipped the ring on her ring finger. It fit. She held her hand at arm's length. "You shouldn't have done this. It's far too expensive a gift."

"Why not buy a ring for my future bride?"

"I hardly know what to say, Rinaldo. Is this a proposal?"

"Not entirely." Rinaldo went down on one knee and looked up at her. He smiled and said, "Rosina, I love you. Will you marry me?" She saw earnest regard in his eyes, and tears welled up in hers. She looked him over as he knelt before her. Thoughts flew through her mind, but he remained silent waiting for her answer. She looked at the ring. She looked around the park, not seeing anything but confirming that this man was real and that she was not dreaming. She made her decision though it would cost her a lifetime.

"Yes, Rinaldo, I will marry you. You make me so happy." He stood up and opened his arms. She entered his embrace and hugged him. He wrapped his arms around her and pressed her close. She melted into his arms and pressed her face against his chest. Tears of joy streamed down her face. He chucked her under the chin, raised her head and kissed her lips gently. Then he kissed her eyes. Her mouth found his and they kissed long and hard. When they parted, he held her trembling hand.

"Rosina, you have just made me the happiest gypsy in New York. Thank you. Now let's shake out our bags for the ducks and find a couple of cups of coffee. It's a little chilly, and I don't want my future bride to catch a cold."

They shook their bags over the pond to empty the remnants of crumbs and walked to the nearest coffee shop where they sat down to enjoy the moment. They were both smiling. Rinaldo was watching her as she thought over what had just happened. Rosina was rubbing her new ring with her thumb.

"It's a diamond!"

"Yes, I know, and it's very beautiful. I can't wait to show it to my mother."

"Hola helped me pick it out, so she has seen it already and approved. She even tried it on herself."

"She knew you were going to propose marriage to me? She never spoke a word about that."

"She said she wasn't sure you were going to accept my proposal. She wanted you to be free to do what you wanted without her seeming to interfere."

"When we're done here, let's drop by to let her know the good news. She's going to want to know when we're getting married. She'll also want to know when we're going to move to Chicago."

"She'll want to move to Chicago too. I did talk that possibility over with her when I took her shopping for your ring. She told me she was excited about the prospect of moving. I told her we'd have adjacent apartments that look out on Lake Michigan. The view is extraordinary in all seasons. The time for the wedding and for you two to move is whenever you feel ready, but I have the date of May 15th next year in mind. Now that we're engaged, we can relax and do our planning."

"Rinaldo, you are so considerate. Hola will want us to have a big family wedding. That will require time to make our guest list and send out invitations. We'll have to consider where the wedding should be done."

"I was thinking we could make it a circus wedding."

"Are you joking?"

"I'm not kidding. We've got family on both sides involved with the circus so they would not have to disrupt their work to attend. Hola liked the idea when I suggested it to her. She launched right in to tell me stories about the circus people in your ancestry."

"We'll see about that when we visit her tonight for dinner. Right now I'm trying to catch my breath. There's so much to think about all at once. Oh, Rinaldo, you've made me happy. I can't remember a time when I felt as relieved and hopeful as I do now." She smiled, and he gently squeezed her hand.

That evening Rinaldo and Rosina broke the good news to Hola at dinner. The roses and red wine that Rinaldo brought for the occasion brightened Hola's dining room and everyone's disposition. Rosina grilled lamb chops and roasted small potatoes. She made a salad from mixed greens. For dessert, she had bought a rhubarb and strawberry pie, which she intended to serve a la mode with vanilla ice cream.

"Just looking at you two being so happy brings back good memories of my engagement and marriage. Rosina, it's about time you made a home for your own family. Rinaldo, tell me how you are going to support Rosina and your children." Hola was always practical, and Rinaldo was ready with an answer that surprised both women.

"Now that we're going to be one family let me tell you what I've been doing in my new job. I come to New York to talk with investors about putting money into my Chicago company's enterprises. When I'm lucky, the investors will wire hundreds of thousands of dollars to my company. My company will put the money to work and give the investors a handsome return. I will earn a big commission."

"What sort of enterprises is your company funding?" Hola asked.

"Circuses, mainly, but a wide range of public entertainments. I was hired by my company because I know the circus business from the inside. No one else in my company really knows everything about what really makes a circus business work. When investors talk with me, they get good answers to all their questions. The investors want to know how their money will be used and how they will get their returns."

"These are tough times, and people don't have a lot of money," Rosina said. "My fortune-telling business ebbs and flows with the economy."

"That's true, Rosina, but no matter how little money people have, they always want to pay for a good time for their whole family. Everyone likes the circus. They like films too, but nothing beats the circus because it's fun for everyone."

"Rinaldo is right, Rosina. The ups and downs in the economy hardly matter for the circuses. I know that because I know the circus business. But Rinaldo, how does your company use the money you get from your rich investors?"

"My company pools the money and funds nearly every aspect of circus operations. A circus might need to buy animals or pay for veterinary services. It might need to buy a new Big Top or equipment. Sometimes my company lends money so that a new circus act can be developed. For example, we paid for the travel expenses of the shortest man and woman in the world to come to America and travel with a circus. We discovered a woman who had a very long beard and paid for her transportation from Africa so she could be a top draw at a circus."

"How do your investors get their returns?" asked Hola, now sitting on the edge of her chair.

She had laid her fork and knife down and held her glass of wine as if it were a talisman.

"Circuses make money with what they buy and the circus pays us back in quarterly payments from their increased revenues. We have finance people who manage all that. We pay our investors ten percent on their money. So if someone invests, say, one hundred thousand dollars, he or she will get back one hundred, ten thousand dollars. Many of our investors decide to reinvest their money repeatedly. Some have made fortunes."

"It sounds like your investors already have fortunes. Do they have to be very rich to invest?"

"Yes, they do. I do presentations in Chicago and harvest investments there, but New York is where the big money can be found. That's why I have to come here routinely. I make my money on commissions for bringing in investments."

"What are your long-term plans, Rinaldo?" Hola asked, apparently satisfied with the young man's ability to provide support for her daughter. Hola always looked beyond the present into the future, and as she always told Rosina, she expected men to be provident.

"I want to make Rosina happy every day. I want to make a big family with her, six children with both boys and girls. One day I want to own the company I'm working for now or own my own circus. It could go either way or both ways at once."

"If you own your company, you might be able to stay in one place. If you own your own circus, you'll always be on the road," Hola observed.

"A lot will depend, Hola, on fate."

"A man makes his fate, Rinaldo."

"A big family can thrive in any case as long as there is love in the home. I'd like to continue telling fortunes," Rosina interjected.

"You can do that, Rosina. I encourage it. Perhaps you should tell our fortunes so we'll both know how things will turn out. I'm serious about this. Besides, it won't hurt to have your talents involved in my business. I agree with your mother that a man makes his fate, but luck plays a role as well." Rinaldo finished his lamb chop and reached for another with his fork. Rosina poured everyone more wine while they digested the ideas they had heard.

"I propose a toast to the newly engaged couple," Hola said, raising her glass of wine. Rinaldo and Rosina touched their glasses against hers, and all drank.

"Hola, we've not set a firm date for the wedding. I've thought about it and May 15th next year looks good for me. We wanted to have your opinion about that before we firmed the commitment."

"We gypsies do not like long engagements, but we do like to have the family members feel they are welcome to come to the weddings," Hola said.

"What if we hold the wedding at the circus that is coming to Chicago next May 15th?"

"Do you want the ceremony to be part of a circus act?" Hola asked with a twinkle in her eye.

"Hahaha. Not at all," Rinaldo answered. "My reasons are practical and personal. I have family in the circus business and so do you. They'll be comfortable in the circus setting. The gypsy camp near the fairground can be used for accommodating out-of-area visitors. With eight months to prepare, all family members who want to attend can make plans in advance. So what do you both think about that?" The women ruminated on this grand idea for a moment. Rosina refilled the wine glasses. Hola responded.

"Rinaldo, I like your idea. Please get together the addresses of the members of your family who should attend. We'll do the same for our family. Rosina and I will design and order the invitations from a printer I know. His work is inexpensive but exquisite. We may get a discount because he comes from gypsy stock. We'll mail the printed invitations out as early as the end of the week after next, provided that we receive the addresses from you."

"Mom, I'm very excited," Rosina said. "The whole family has not been together since we buried papa. Now everyone has changed and so many new children have been born. It will be so good to see everyone. We'll have time to make my wedding dress and plan our move to Chicago."

"That's true. At some point we'll be moving to Chicago permanently, won't we, Rinaldo?"

"Yes, Hola, and I already have rented the perfect place—two adjacent apartments overlooking Lake Michigan."

"Chicago has bitter, cold winters."

"Yes, it has very cold winters with icy winds coming down from the Arctic Circle. Chicago is not called the Windy City for nothing."

"Brrrr. I'm not looking forward to the winters there. Ice and snow are treacherous."

"Mom, New York is icy and snowy in the winter too."

"I suppose you're right, Rosina. Anyway, you'll have a big, warm husband to keep you warm at night." Rosina blushed, and Rinaldo took her hand and kissed it.

"Mom, it's late. Rinaldo will have to get back to his hotel. He's leaving for Chicago early tomorrow morning."

"Future son-in-law, I thank you from the bottom of my heart. Rosina's life will now be complete. Looking at you two makes my heart sing. Goodnight."

The next day after Rinaldo had departed, Rosina and her mother began planning for the circus wedding in earnest. The printer Hola knew did give them a deep discount, and his ideas improved their invitations. He printed not only the invitations but RSVP returns. The package of two hundred and fifty engraved invitations and RSVP responses were ready within five business days, as promised. Rinaldo sent one hundred names and addresses for his family. Hola and Rosina drew up a list of one hundred-fifty names and addresses for their own family. As Hola planned, the invitations were mailed at the end of the second week after Rinaldo's departure.

The mother and daughter then planned the wedding dress. They selected the materials and threads. The model for the dress was Hola's own bridal costume. The two women worked for four weeks to bring the dress together. It was white, as befitted a virgin bride. It was daring, as befitted a gypsy bride. Rosina worried about losing or gaining weight before the nuptial day, but Hola urged her daughter to think of her future husband and not about whether she was going to fit perfectly into her gown. Hola was pleased when Rinaldo wired money to defray the expenses of the printing and the dress. He had the good grace to say that since Rosina's father was no longer alive, his contributions should be viewed as supplementary.

Through all the time of preparations, Rosina continued to read fortunes and provide advice as a reader-advisor. She continued to ply her trade in dreams and speculations though her greatest concern was, for a change, for her own future. This concern was reinforced by the deluge of responses she and Hola received for the wedding.

Not only did she receive responses from the one hundred-fifty addressees, they also received responses from another hundred gypsies who wanted to be included even though they had not received formal invitations. Hola and Rosina had a heated discussion about this unforeseen event.

"Mom, we simply have to allow everyone who is related to the people who received invitations to come. Didn't we want this to be a time for us to know the new arrivals in the family?"

"Rosina, some of these inquiries are from wastrels and parasites. They just want to have free food and drink. Some of them are violent people. If we let them attend, they'll want to bring their families too."

"I'd rather admit more who want to come than to leave someone out who we might want to know later."

"Okay, we can pick and choose, but you'll have to let Rinaldo know about the increase in attendees. He is paying for the festivities, and it's partly his decision too."

Rosina wrote to Rinaldo about the additional hundred-odd attendees. He responded that he welcomed as many as she and Hola desired. He wrote back that circus people should be given precedence for business reasons. Rosina reviewed the list and discovered that the majority of the outliers were circus people.

"Mom, we simply must include any circus people who want to attend the wedding.

Rinaldo likes the idea. He's paying. So there you go."

"Circus people are always looking for a free meal."

"Rinaldo's business is to help circuses. This fits perfectly."

As a result, Hola and Rosina included circus people, and those invited their friends and associates. Before long, three hundred additional names had been added to the attendees, not including wives, children, and cousins.

Rinaldo wrote, "We can accommodate all the additional people. The character of the event is going to change a little, but we can manage it."

"Rinaldo, what do you mean by 'the character of the event is going to change a little'?"

"Dearest Rosina, my company will pay for our entire wedding. If circus people are going to attend, they want them to perform at the wedding. This will be great for business and for the individual performers too. My company is inviting the best reporters in Chicago from all the media to cover the event. Open the gates and let all the circus people come. If you don't mind having our marriage ceremony getting publicity, we're fine. So what do you think?"

"Rinaldo," Rosina responded, "Whatever you decide, we'll do. Hola likes the idea of including the circus people as long as the company is paying."

Rinaldo and Rosina's Chicago circus wedding became a cause célèbre and took on a life of its own. The New York and Chicago papers gave the event full play. Pictures of the bride and groom were published well in advance. The media frenzy that resulted caused Rinaldo's company to expand the event to include its A-list prospects. Circus performers from around the world decided that the wedding was a venue they simply had to attend. A new deluge of would-be attendees flowed into Rinaldo's company. The attendee list swelled to over one thousand attendees, and Rinaldo's company reveled in the prospect.

Now Rosina and Hola were working furiously on the costumes for the children who were expected to attend the wedding. All Rosina's female family members were to be bridesmaids. Hola designed the costumes, and the bridesmaids' measurements were requested and received. Rinaldo was informed of the potential additional costs, and his company wired the money directly to Hola. Mother and daughter worked twenty hours a day to sew the garments that they sent to the families of the bridesmaids. Some alterations were necessary, and those were accomplished. Being gypsies, the parents of the bridesmaids took a cue from Hola's design and manufactured costumes for the men and women alike to match.

Special requests to accommodate the elder members of the families came in. These were forwarded to Rinaldo, whose company was happy to accommodate. Several of the prospective attendees were over one hundred years old. An investigative reporter was engaged to cover this important aspect of the event. So former famous circus people had their professional lives reviewed in contemporary society pages. Several bearded ladies and three animal tamers were interviewed about their past adventures in the circus life. Rinaldo's company, realizing the advertising bonanza this represented, looked for other angles that might bring additional investments to the firm. They sent telegraph notices to their talent scouts around the world that talent was welcome at the circus wedding. They promised visibility and the prospect of fame for all who answered the call.

From Russia came word of a seven-foot-tall woman who had been found fully nude, outrunning horses in the wild. She was captured and transported to Chicago. Likewise, five Watusi women warriors were enticed to Chicago by the prospect of wealth beyond anything they could imagine in their native country. Not only were the smallest dwarfs in the world, but their seven nearest competitors were invited to the wedding, all expenses paid. Exotic animal acts came too, among them a woman with her twenty-foot anaconda, a man who had tamed a wildebeest, a family that had domesticated chimpanzees and a falconer who sported a brace of hunting falcons. The circus wedding was expanding rapidly, and Rinaldo's company saw another opportunity in monetizing the event.

Tickets went on sale for the circus extravaganza of the decade. The one dollar price of admission was only the beginning. Each event had its own price, and books of tickets for assorted events were available for sale. The wedding was excluded from the for-sale events though some higher ups in Rinaldo's company were resentful that it had not been properly monetized. Rinaldo wrote Rosina that he was now in charge of a new unit in his company called, "Circus Extravaganzas." His own wedding was to be the prototype of many future such events if it was profitable enough. That way Rinaldo became an overnight impresario. He also became the focal point for all disputes involving his venue.

On St. Valentine's Day Rinaldo managed to visit New York to do a blitz of potential investors for his Circus Extravaganzas. He saw Hola and Rosina one night for dinner during his visit.

"I managed to break free from the rat race for one meal with you, and I'm delighted for once not to be hounded about my projects."

"Rinaldo, your company has stolen our wedding," Rosina said sadly.

"Rosina, don't blame Rinaldo. His company has re-factored the wedding, but that hasn't changed the important thing: your marriage. You wanted to see your family, and you'll see them. Rinaldo, you'll see your family also."

"Rosina is right, Hola. Our wedding has been co-opted by my company."

"But Rinaldo, your fame, and your new position are good for your career," Rosina said helpfully.

"That's true, my dear, but I didn't want our wedding to get out of our control. They way things have gone, I cannot put the genie back in the bottle now. Will you forgive me?"

"What's to forgive? I decided to expand our guest list to include the others. I will live with my decision. If we can bolster your career by our circus wedding, we'll both gain by it."

"Listen to her, Rinaldo. This kind of chance comes once in a lifetime. Seize the opportunity by the forelock. I do like this fillet mignon you brought us. It's delicious."

"I'm glad you like it. The company wanted us to have the best of everything now that we've created such a bevy of good advertising."

"Rinaldo, I understand that you've become a troubleshooter in your new job."

"That's right, Hola. Any problems with our circus wedding come directly to me. I have to solve them all satisfactorily. The press is dogging my every move."

"What kind of problems have you solved?"

"The woman with the anaconda lost her snake somewhere in Toledo. I had to find the snake amid a local panic and restore it to the woman. Don't laugh, Rosina, the snake was twenty feet long. I found it in a cattle feeding pen wrapped around a calf it had taken a fancy to. Then there was the woman from the Russian taiga. She decided she did not like her accommodations, so she went out one evening to see the Chicago nightlife. Of course, she wore no clothing. So she was arrested for indecent exposure. The police were baffled that she seemed not to notice the extremely cold weather. They had chased her across the frozen lake in a Jeep that spun and twirled on the ice before they finally netted the woman. I had to pay her bail and shut down the media's attempt to publish the escape story in the tabloids."

"Rinaldo, this is too funny. What other problems have you solved in your new role?" Hola was doubled over in laughter, but she recovered as he continued with his tales.

"You've heard about the proverbial barrel full of monkeys. Well, I had to deal with more than a barrel full of chimpanzees. As you may know, an angry chimp can be most uncivilized. They were housed in a cage that was much too small for them. They took umbrage and used their own wet feces as projectiles against anyone who approached their cage. I had to supervise the construction of a much larger accommodation. Then the chimps refused to make the transition to it. They had become used to their cramped quarters, particularly to its smell. So I used the new cage for the wildebeest and left instructions for the maintenance crew to hose down the chimps and their cage each morning. So far that has worked out, but the chimps still throw their feces."

"Do you have any bear acts coming?"

"Hola's asking because our people once kept bears."

"Your grandfather brought his bear from the Old Country. He was a magnificent animal, a great money maker until the day he died."

"We do have four bears, but only two are worth telling about. One is a fifteen-foot polar bear. It loves the cold, but it has an enormous appetite. It ate one of the circus seals. Blood was everywhere. I had to find livestock that would satisfy the polar bear's voracity. The other was a grizzly bear. No one can tame those grizzlies. The bear escaped and terrorized the city. The police shot the bear with a tranquilizer gun outside a supermarket where it had decided to feast on the meats in the meat counter. By the time I arrived on the scene, the police were trying to hoist the huge carcass into a Paddy Wagon with a wire line on a winch."

"Did you have any trouble with your bearded ladies?" Hola asked.

"I never figured that those ladies would be randy, but they were. They would go after anything in pants, me included."

"Hahaha. I can see it now. How did you escape them?"

"I didn't...I'm just kidding. I simply threatened to have them restrained and shaved. That would have ended their livelihood—until, of course, they grew their beards out again. Their beards are all over one foot in length. I don't think any man could compete with them in a beard growing contest."

"Rinaldo, is everything ready for our wedding in the middle of all this circus activity?" Rosina asked when she recovered from her bout of laughter over the bearded ladies.

"Darling, everything is on track for our ceremony. Hola, have all the bridesmaids' costumes been completed?"

"Yes, they have. The bridesmaids' families have made clothing in a similar style for all their attendees. The only things we now lack are the flowers."

"The company will pay for the flowers. Every florist shop in Chicago will be contributing something for the wedding. All the bridesmaids will be carrying baskets of flowers. The area for the ceremony will be lined with potted plants and flowers. Palm trees, proteas and other exotic flowers and trees will be included. The bride will carry flowers including two dozen perfect red roses. Since the ceremony will be in the evening, it will be lighted by candles."

"It all sounds so beautiful," Hola said.

"The wedding, as I said, is ready with the exception of a few details that we'll manage as we go along. The surprise I have for you is the honeymoon."

"Oh, with all the commotion, I forgot all about the honeymoon," said Rosina.

"We're going to Niagara Falls on the Canadian side for three days—if Hola can manage things while we're away. Hola, you'll be in your new apartment overlooking Lake Michigan then. I've got a fine young woman named Helga coming. She'll cook your meals and help with the cleaning."

"Rinaldo, you are always so considerate. I'll be able to manage fine even without the help. What's the plan for the moves?"

"You and Rosina will take the train to Chicago. You'll arrive two days before the wedding. I'll meet you at the station and take you to your apartment. You'll both stay in the apartment until the wedding. That afternoon you'll be escorted to the circus for the ceremony. Hola, we'll see that you get back to your apartment after the wedding before we take off on our honeymoon."

"There are so many little details to attend to."

"Yes, and I want you to let me know if you need anything at all. The melee of the extravaganza has been set up to run pretty much on its own. My chief concern now is our wedding. That's the whole reason for everything else."

"Rinaldo, this toast is for you for having thought of everything," Rosina said as she raised her wineglass. Hola drank with her, and Rinaldo shook his head.

"Rosina, why don't you do your magic and look into our future."

"Everything is going so well, should we press our luck?"

"Darling, it's when everything is going well that we most need to have our fortune's told. Seriously, it's time for that."

"Your future husband is right, Rosina. Why not do it right now before he returns to Chicago?"

"All right, if you two help me clear the table, I'll be able to finish early and set up for the reading."

Rosina decided to use a combination of palm reading and Tarot to divine their future. She saw in Rinaldo's palm a strong lifeline. The Tarot revealed a fortune and happiness. All having been positive so far, she ventured further by envisioning with a flame that burned in a red candle. There she saw something disconcerting. She saw the face of the man she had gone to Chicago to see in the first place. She tried to avoid it, but the face was insistent. Rosina mentioned only that she had seen a face that could cause trouble for the wedding. She was not specific.

"You see long life, fortune, and happiness. What more could we wish for, Rosina?" Rinaldo was all smiles.

"The future is mysterious," was all that Rosina could say.

"There's nothing mysterious about life, fortune, and happiness, Rosina," Hola told her daughter.

Rosina was pensive, but she decided to break her own study by changing the subject to her makeup.

"Do you want me to come as a painted doll or as a natural gypsy?" she asked her future husband.

"As long as you are there and say yes at the wedding, my day will be complete. You can wear as much makeup and jewelry as you like."

"Rinaldo, she will be wearing the same jewelry as I wore when I married, except for the diamond engagement ring you gave her. She'll have rings on her fingers."

"Yes, Mama, and bells on my toes, and I shall have music wherever I go."

"Speaking of music, Rosina, we'll have gypsy musicians for our reception after the wedding. We'll dance wild dances and sing. My company is providing a barrel of wine so there will be plenty to drink. Whole roasted boar will assure that there will be plenty to eat. The feast will feed a multitude."

"It will have to. At the last count, we'll have fifteen hundred people attending."

"Add to those my entire company from the president to the stock boys."

"That's news."

"I only learned about it a few days ago. The company has decided that the wedding is going to substitute for our annual company outing. I'll have to be on my best behavior because my boss will be there watching me."

"What's next?" Rosina wondered out loud.

"What's next is that I have to go. Thank you both for a tremendous evening. I think we're ready to start the circus show whenever we like."

"As long as you are there, all will go well, my love."

"Rosina, don't worry. I'll be there, and all will go well." Rinaldo kissed Rosina gently on the lips. He kissed Hola on the forehead and looked into her eyes. "Sleep well. I'll be waiting for you both in Chicago."

Rinaldo returned to Chicago and the rat race. He wrote letters every other day and numbered them to assure that they all were received. When she received the letters, Rosina replied by return post. She felt almost overwhelmed because she still kept up her fortune telling business while she worked with Hola on the thousand remaining details for the wedding.

In a hiatus between appointments, she was looking out the window of her office into the late afternoon sunshine when someone knocked on her door. She answered and there she saw standing the man she had gone to Chicago to find. He had not changed from her memory of him.

"Rosina, it's me, Robert. I have to explain why I was not in Chicago when you came to visit me. I'll only be a minute, I promise. I know all about your planned marriage. I don't want to intrude. May I come in?"

"I have an appointment in fifteen minutes. I can talk with you until then. Come in and sit down." She gestured to a chair by her viewing table. He sat down and she sat down across from him.

"This is a surprise. I thought you were dead. I didn't know what to think, really. You look well."

"I may look well now, but I've been through an ordeal that scares me just to recount it. I have to tell you why I was away. I've felt so rotten. I'd like for you to forgive me, but I know I don't deserve it."

"Go on, please," Rosina told the earnest man. She recalled envisioning him when she told Rinaldo's fortune. She remembered how his face had been such a surprise then. Now she marveled that the same face was before her speaking now.

"I was struck by a car while I was walking on the street down by the El. I blacked out and was taken to the hospital emergency room. I did not become conscious for two weeks while the doctors speculated whether I would recover. Finally, when I did come to, I remembered nothing of the past—absolutely nothing. I didn't remember you or where I lived or my name. I was institutionalized and put under observation by a battery of psychiatrists who tried to bring my memory back. For two years they worked on me using every trick they knew. Finally, I was out walking on the grounds of the institution when I collapsed. The doctors found me and conveyed me to my room where I lay unconscious for another two weeks. This time, I awakened to find my memory had returned. It had not returned in pieces. It returned intact. I was frantic because I thought you were coming to see me. I now knew who I was and where I lived. All I could think of was you because I love you. I have only loved you, just as I wrote you in those letters. Then I read the papers and I knew that you were at the center of the circus wedding. I saw your picture. I did not dare come to you because you had gone well beyond the point where I had left you."

"So why are you here now?"

"A few days ago I felt you were calling to me. I saw your face before me. You look the same as you do right now. You have the same shocked expression. I just had to find you and see you one more time before you married. I thought you loved me once. I could not be sure whether you were going to be married as a default to me or in revenge for my having disappeared at a critical point in our relationship."

"So here we are. Robert, what do you want from me now?"

"First, I want you to forgive me."

"There's nothing to forgive. What happened, you did not do purposely. It was an accident. How can I fault you for that?"

"I'm very much relieved. I couldn't go on living if you were angry with me."

"I'm much relieved as well. Knowing you are alive makes me happy. I once wanted to reform my whole life around you. Yes, I loved you. You were the love of my life, my first love."

"That answers the second reason that I came. To have you confirm that you loved me is reassuring. What we had was real and good. It was like a heaven that suddenly I was deprived of."

"I felt that way too. Now it is too late to turn the clock back."

"Is it really too late? Are you fully committed to proceed with this wedding? Why it's become the media extravaganza of the time."

"That part means nothing to me."

"I thought it might not because you always were so real to me. Your love was substantial in a world of hucksterism and fraud."

"I felt the same about you. The fact that you're here bears out the truth of it."

"How is Hola?"

"She's doing well. We're both going to Chicago. We'll live there after the wedding."

"I'm living in Chicago too. Maybe we'll see one another there. I hope so."

"Stop this. Right now. Robert, I've given you the time you asked for. Now you must leave me. When I come to Chicago, you will *not* seek me out. You will *not* fantasize about our former relationship. You will forget me and find another match. I've made a promise. I wear this ring." She held out her hand with the diamond ring, and he took it gently. She did not withdraw her hand.

"I hear you, Rosina, but your eyes tell me something from your heart. Don't look away, my darling." He leaned towards her slowly and kissed her on the lips. She did not pull away. She kissed him back. Then she stood abruptly and went to the door.

"You really must go now. Please go. Don't speak. Forget what we've just done. I have a customer coming." As if to confirm this, a knock sounded on the door. She opened the door to find her customer, a middle-class woman of middle age holding a miniature poodle against her coat.

"I'm sorry. We do have an appointment now, don't we?"

"Yes, of course, Mrs. Abernathy. Please come in. My client was just leaving. Thank you, sir, for coming. I hope you'll have a safe journey home. Goodbye."

Rosina closed the door after the lady had taken her seat and the young man had departed. The woman was trying to discover whether her husband was being unfaithful to her. Rosina composed herself to look into the future. Her heart was not in her job, but she was a professional.

"Mrs. Abernathy, I'm afraid I have some bad news for you."

The woman broke down in tears. Her poodle started howling in her lap. Rosina handed the woman a handkerchief and let her sob. There was no consolation. In fact, Rosina observed to herself, the truth was written all over the woman. It had taken four sessions to put together the vision that Rosina had elicited. This was the first time that the woman had broken down and cried. Rosina lost her composure and began to weep as well. She knew what the woman was feeling, but her feeling was empathy, not sympathy. The two women wept together for five minutes. Then they stopped.

"I need to know what comes next."

"Be calm. Relax. Breathe. Empty your head of all thoughts. Now, what do you see?"

"I see my husband's face."

"You're sure?"

"Yes, yes, I'm sure. It's him. There's no mistake."

"Go home then. Forget you ever came here. Forget and forgive what your husband has done. Love him so hard that it would break his heart if he knew that you had any inkling of what he has done."

The woman opened her purse and took out a ten dollar bill. She placed it in the little jar on the fortune teller's desk. She put Rosina's handkerchief on the table beside the jar. Rising to her feet, she adjusted her dog and her purse so that she could walk to the door.

"Thank you, Rosina. You've been most understanding. Would you mind awfully if I came again sometime."

"Not at all, Mrs. Abernathy. I'm glad I could help. Just call me to schedule another appointment. Goodbye for now."

When she closed the door, Rosina stood with her back to the door for a moment and breathed deeply. When she felt confident that she could move without fainting or falling, she cleaned up her room. She was finished with her business for the day. Now she had to walk home to help Hola prepare dinner. She decided to stop by the butcher's shop on the way to pick up two chops. It had been a trying day. She was not sure what she should do about the apparition that had come in the form of her lost love Robert.

Rosina prepared Hola's dinner like an automaton. She did not chatter with her mother as she normally did. Hola knew her daughter's moods well. She knew something important had happened. She waited to see whether Rosina would tell what was on her mind rather than probing her daughter about her day. Only when the food was on the table and the two sat down to eat did Hola break the silence.

"You're awfully quiet this evening, Rosina. Is something wrong?"

"Oh, I'm sorry Mama. I had an unusually busy day at the office."

"It's more than that, isn't it? Please pass the potatoes and tell me about it. Is it about Rinaldo?"

"Mama, you remember the boy Robert I went to see in Chicago, but he was gone?"

"Of course, I remember Robert. He's the reason you came into contact with Rinaldo. Without him, you wouldn't have found the man you're going to marry."

"When I was telling Rinaldo's fortune, Robert appeared to me in a vision."

"All right. Sometimes it happens that our past intrudes on the present. Do you think you saw his ghost?"

"If it was a ghost, I saw it again when he came through my office door today. He had the same face as the figure in my vision."

"Was it really real, or were you hallucinating?"

"It was as real as you are. Robert wanted to tell me he was sorry he was not there to meet me in Chicago when I came to find him. He wanted me to absolve him from his guilt. He wanted to know how I felt about him. He said he loved me. I told him that at the time I loved him too. The man touched me. He kissed me. Mama, I let him kiss me! I responded by kissing him back!"

"Then what happened?" Hola asked this in a deadpan tone to elicit her daughter's response without intimidating or influencing her.

"I told Robert to stop and just go away. I told him that when we go to Chicago, I want him to stay away from us. Before I could say anything else, my customer arrived. Robert left. When my work was done, I closed up the office and came here, stopping only to buy these chops. He was nowhere in sight."

"Robert just showed up at your door. I see. Did he explain why he never got in touch with you? You left him notes as I recall."

"He said he had gotten total amnesia from an accident with a car. He could not even remember his name or where he lived. He couldn't remember me or anything about our plans."

"And what made him remember again?"

"He said he had a fall at an institution where he was being treated. His memory came back in a whoosh. He remembered me. He felt guilty about not having been in touch. Then he saw the reports of the circus wedding."

"That should have clarified for him that you had moved on."

"He said he still loved me. I think he wanted to know whether I still felt the same about him before the marriage."

"How do you feel about Robert now?"

"Mama, when you love someone to the bottom of your soul, you don't forget him. At least, I don't."

"You made a promise to Rinaldo. You are engaged to be married on May 15th. Has seeing Robert again changed those things?"

"Mama, I showed him the ring. I cut him off. I clarified where I stood."

"You did those things, but was it your head or your heart that did the clarifying?"

"Oh, Mama, Robert looked into my eyes and I responded. He was the man in the vision, and I think my mind called him to come to me. He told me that he had seen a vision of me just like the one I had seen of him. I think it was at the same time. Now I feel confused."

"Rosina, I can't tell you what to do. You will have to sort out your feelings and chart a way forward. If your heart lies with this other man Robert, you will have to decide whether to keep on course with the plan for your marriage or to break off your engagement and fly to your former love. Do you or do you not love Rinaldo?"

"Yes, I love Rinaldo, and I will marry him as I promised to do."

"Rosina, do you love Robert?"

"Mama, I used to love him, and the memory of that love has never faded. I have no idea what might happen if I left Rinaldo at this stage."

"You told Rinaldo his fortune right at this table and saw the things that would make anyone happy."

"Yes, I did. I just don't understand."

"Understand what?"

"Why did I push beyond the Tarot to envision? Why did I see what I saw? Why did that act like a conjuration to bring me face to face with my past love? Why did I kiss back when Robert's lips touched mine? Why was it so hard for me to tell him never to seek me out again or speak to me?"

"I can't answer those questions, Rosina. Why don't you finish your dinner? Then clean up and go home and think about everything. Sleep can sometimes bring the answers."

"I know you're right, Mama. I'm just afraid of what the answers will tell me."

"How many times have you told fortunes that you knew would cause your customers pain?"

"Many times. I've told you about some of those instances. Some of my customers have committed suicide and some have murdered on account of what I said to them."

"A person's fortune always brings pain even when it portends good."

"You always told me that. The reason, you said, was that a fortune cuts us off from all the other possibilities that might have been."

"Precisely so. Come now; eat your chop before it gets any colder. Tell me about the other things that happened at your office today."

Rosina told Hola about Mrs. Abernathy, whose husband had been unfaithful. She told her the advice she gave the distraught woman.

"You gave her good advice. Do you think she'll take it?"

"Sometimes I give advice and don't ever know the outcome."

"If you were in that woman's place, would you have taken your advice?"

"I don't know. I just don't know."

That night Rosina had a dream of feeding the ducks with Rinaldo. She remembered distinctly his dropping on one knee and proposing marriage to her. She felt warm all over at the recollection. She saw his face clearly. He was smiling up at her, waiting for her answer to his proposal. The world stood still for a moment before she had said yes. In her dream, she said yes all over again.

The next morning Rosina felt good. She telephoned her mother and told her, "Everything will be all right."

Five days later Rosina received a package in the mail at her office. Its return address was in Chicago. When she opened the package, she found all the letters she had sent Robert. She found his copies of the pictures that documented their past. The picture that brought her to the point of tears was the one of Robert and her feeding the swans in the pond. Along with the letters and pictures was a one-page note:

Dear Rosina,

Thank you for seeing me one last time. I apologize for any pain I might have caused you, but I had to ask your forgiveness and I had to know the truth about your feelings. You have forgiven me, and I know the truth. I wish you long life, a blessed marriage, and happiness. I will never forget you, but I must return your letters and pictures because they bring me too much pain. As a fortune teller, you know the pain that sometimes comes with knowledge of the truth. Know this: I love you. I have always loved you. I will always love you. Fate played a cruel trick, so here we are. As you requested, I will not bother you again, ever.

Love, Robert

Rosina was surprised that she did not weep. Instead, she concluded that her path ahead was charted. Robert belonged to her past. Rinaldo was her future. Today she had four customers on her schedule. She carefully replaced the letters and pictures back in the package in which they had come. She laid the package on an empty bookshelf. Then she went to her desk and arranged her props. She pulled the shades so that the room was dark. Hola always taught that darkness was the realm where truth was hidden. She thought about calling her mother just to touch base and confirm what she had said earlier. She resolved that she did not need to do that now. Tonight was soon enough for the confirmation. Her mind and heart were in synchronicity. Without distractions, she could see clearly.

Searching for a Magician

Vanessa Essler Carlson

"How does mine look?" He sat in the seat across from me. "I have always been curious. I can only visualize the energies of others as I am sure is the same with you. A vivid blue, right?"

I lit my pipe and inhaled deeply. Somehow I felt it would make me appear calmer even though his presence set fire to my navel. Odd that a man I had loathed long before I knew him would be the first to share the sight with me. I had so many questions. What exactly are the energies? A person's life? The soul? Was there meaning behind the colors? I felt the taste of bile rise to the back of my throat.

"A mix of colors, actually. All moving," I said.

The triangle of hair beneath his lip lengthened as he grinned. "'Tis the same as yours then. Quite fascinating." He removed the top hat and rubbed his bald crown. "John Branton. I have been waiting a rather long time for the chance to meet you. I assume you know who I am."

The colors surrounding his body shifted furiously. The letters pulsed in and out of focus. I read them aloud. "Markel Baker."

He nodded. "My, my… aren't you a clever card."

The last of the patrons sloshed their way out of the pub. They knocked over a few chairs and slammed the door as they left. The barmaid set down her bucket and newspaper to put the furniture upright. She went to cleaning the inside windows. A pungent vinegar smell burst from the bucket as she dipped the paper. She wiped it around the glass a bit before scowling at us.

"Closing time, blokes."

The bodice of her dress was loose. She had to adjust the shoulders with a thin, pale arm so as not to slip out. The edges of her energy were grey and tattering. Whatever ailment had taken hold of her was rapid. She likely only had a few months left. From the looks of what was left of her energy, she had probably been a golden hue in her health. The same golden I had always thought Madeline McKrauss had been. She was the first of Markel Baker's victims. Well known as a lively barmaid; robust, and able to carry ten pints without a tray. The night we examined the body, all the color was gone. Death left a trail of energy. Sometimes the color was a solid streak or wispy tentacles reaching out. They stained the air around the corpse for days. McKrauss was still warm, but there was only a void surrounding her. No blood. No bruises. The woman had simply fallen over without breath. Over the years, I had encountered dozens of such deaths. I knew they were all from the same man, the same shadow I had chased in the streets behind Burrough Manor after he had taken their daughter. All this time fleeing, then he decides to strike up a conversation as if we were old mates.

"We won't be long. Just a moment alone." I called through my smoke.

"Very well, constable." She tossed the newspaper on a table and left.

I smoothed my mustache with my thumb and index finger. "Why?"

"Why, brother? Not how? Ah, so you are able to steal energies as well."

I slammed my fist down on the table. "That was an accident."

The triangle of dark hair beneath his lip widened to a nearly impossible extreme. Setting his elbows on the table, he perched his chin on folded hands. I puffed on my pipe while he waited.

"Not willing to elaborate?"

"Why?" I repeated.

"Not a man of many words, are you?" He leaned in closer. "Why? A fine question. The world is a harsh place. Famine. Storm. Hell, another plague could descend upon us at any moment. What if we knew of such hardships before they occurred? What would you say to that power?"

"So you want power then?" I sucked on the pipe. The gritty taste of warm ash hit my tongue. I knocked the pipe clean in the ashtray. "You kill for power."

"Power? No, not like you are thinking. I am speaking of the greater good. For the sake of the advancement of man."

"You're a liar and a murderer."

He shook his head. "You are not hearing me. I have made sacrifices for the betterment of all." He pulled a deck of cards from his coat. "I will show you, brother. Here. Man's salvation."

He fanned the deck before me. A kaleidoscope of energies emanating from them.

The burning that had taken residence in my navel moved to the base of my throat.

"Cards? You took all those people's lives and put them in cards?" I stammered.

"Anyone, in particular, you would like to see?" He shuffled the deck from hand to hand.

Heat spread through my chest watching him flip victims around as playthings. I didn't even realize I had hissed out "Madeline McKrauss," until he had placed her card face up on the table. She was rosy-cheeked and smiling. Hair pinned up in a perfect bun. Five full pint glasses in each hand ready for some table of customers. The whole scene radiated peacock blue, not the gold I had long dreamt she was. Every inch of my flesh was scalding. At the bottom of the card in a fancy font was scribed *X of Cups*.

"A tarot deck," I said in sheer astonishment.

"Precisely. You can envision it now, surely. With such power, any reading from this deck becomes immensely accurate. The future can be foreseen. Wars averted. Crops spared from wildfires." He stroked the length of Madeline McKrauss before returning her to the deck. "The few will save the many."

"And you plan no profit for yourself?"

His lip curled back slightly exposing a sliver of his teeth. "Do I not deserve some compensation? Years of work in the name of humanity."

"You are nothing more than a selfish murderer. All those deaths for money and power." I wiped the sweat from the back of my neck; either I was burning from the inside out or the erratic motion of his energies was heating the pub.

The downturn crescent mouth expanded to expose fangs. I wanted them to be long and sharp so I could further prove his vileness, but they were merely human in appearance. Baker went through the deck in a frenzy and then slammed a card face down on the table. This one was unlike the others with a thick void engulfing the space rather than any energy.

"I shall prove myself then. This is the final card. The last one needed to complete the deck." He flipped it up.

Blank, save the text at the bottom: *The Magician*. My stomach compressed. I was staring into an abyss. Empty chains reaching out for a captive.

"The Magician is one who uses his magic to change the world. Magic, such as we have." His eyes became narrow and I thought I saw fear run across him as he stared down at the card. "For this to work, for the world to change, this card needs a life. One of us is going in that card, brother."

The fire within me went out and suddenly my blood ran icy. "What?"

"It must be one of us. The energy of a magician that is. I would prefer it was you, of course, but the deck must be completed." Pearls of perspiration were forming on the skin of his scalp. "I am sure you recall how to push energies from your little accident, yes? Therefore, let us duel."

He centered the card an equal distance between us on the table.

"You're a monster."

"On the count of three, my brother. One…"

Sweat pooled along my collar bone. Teeth clenched. Two pairs of fists pressed down hard on either end of the table.

"Two…"

The promise of bondage betwixt us. Gaping. Hungry.

"Three."

Soothsayer

Evelyn M. Zimmer

"But Mamma, there is too much to learn," Lily's frustration caused her to pout.

"You must be a changeling," her mother admonished.

"What's a changeling?" her daughter asked.

"Tsk, that question proves you're not my child. It's what we get when we swap out the bad babies for the gadje," her mother teased. "Now, start counting those staves again."

This wasn't the first time Lily heard her mother say that and knew she was teasing, but she stuck out her tongue anyway. "One, two, three…sixteen, seventeen, Momma, how many is there supposed to be?" Lily sighed, mimicking her mother perfectly, as she tried to make sure that no two staves had the same markings as she tried to count them.

"Twenty-four staves, Lily. Twenty-four staves to a set of runes," she told her daughter for the fourth time that morning as she carved more staves.

"When is Papa coming back?" Lily asked.

"When he is done." The matter of fact answer failed to appease her daughter, and Lala set her carving knives aside, wiped her hands on her skirt and picked up her frustrated six-year-old. "You need to learn to count Lily. You are too old to not be helping the family." Lala placed her chin atop her daughter's head and cuddled her close for several moments. She could smell the sunshine in the dark curls and wondered when she would no longer be able to hold her child in her lap.

Lily began to squirm the moment she heard the distant jingle of the horse harness. "Papa! Papa is back!" she squealed as only six-year-olds can do.

Lala sighed deeply as she watched her youngest child disappear down the lane to meet her father. "Ion, fetch more wood, the fire is dying." Lala directed her eldest son as if ordering a servant, her matter of fact tone would brook no argument.

"Yes, Momma." Ion was glad for a reason to not be present when his father came into camp. He was still smarting from the altercation he had with the boys in the town and didn't want to listen to his father lecture him again.

"Rosa put the water on for tea, your Papa is back." Lala's middle child was compliant and always tried to please her mother, yet somehow managed to never know if she succeeded.

"Lala, come! See what wonders I've procured!" her husband laughed as he neared the camp with Lily jumping about him.

"It better be silver," Lala muttered under her breath as she turned around and plastered a resigned smile on her face.

The sack Besnik laid on the makeshift wooden table landed with a thud that earned Lala's interest. "Open, open," he prodded.

"What is this foolishness?" trying to sound stern, Lala couldn't hide the twinkle in her eye.

"You tell me," he laughed.

Tugging on the drawstring of the sack she peeked inside, then opened it wider and spilled the contents onto the table. "Oh Nik, you squandered our silver on a bird? Ion snares them all the time, why would you do that?" Lala nearly cried at the uselessness of her man with coin.

"No, no tears, my beautiful wife," he cajoled, "for I did not spend coin on the goose. It was a gift from the butcher in the town." His pride caused his chest to puff out a bit.

"Why? Gadje do not give gifts to Romani. Did you steal this husband?" Lala was getting ready for a full blown argument when he stayed her with a smile.

"Wife, do not shame me in front of our daughters. I did not steal the goose, the butcher's wagon threw a wheel and I helped him fix it. He rewarded me with the goose. We are safe, we do not have to move anytime soon. Now, make me some tea." He shooed her towards the campfire as he reached for the goose and made the bill 'quack' for the amusement of his little star, his Lily.

"Papa, what's around your neck?" Lily spied the small pouch as it slipped from beneath the neckline of his shirt.

Placing the tea on the table before her husband, Lala arched her brow in query. "Well, answer the child," she said.

"That is something that will surely make your mother smile my little star," he teased as he withdrew it and placed it gently next to his cup.

Lala opened the pouch and dumped the contents into her palm. Her eyes grew questioning as she opened the folded piece of paper even as she counted the coins. "What is this?"

"Read it my beauty," he winked.

Lala read it twice to be sure, it was an advertisement for an apprentice. "I do not understand, what does this have to do with us? The Baroness wants an apprentice to assist the local healer. We know nothing of healing the gadje way."

"Apprentice means they are willing to teach, why not have Rosa learn a trade that will allow her to mix in all of society?" he quietly asked.

"Rosa? Our Rosa, a healer? No." Lala shook her head and turned her back on her husband to compose herself.

"It's her chance for a stable, settled life Lala, not always moving, not always in danger—"

"What is wrong with our life? We get to see the world on our terms, we meet new people, we learn new things, we—" she fired back.

"It's been settled wife. Call Rosa over." Suddenly Beznik was not her loyal, loving husband, but the head of the clan, and she knew when she was beaten. Three little words silenced her. *It's been settled.*

"Rosa, your Papa needs you," Lala choked the words out as she passed her daughter, then ran into the woods to find Ion.

****

The spring turned to summer and Rosa awoke to the rooster calling another day. She couldn't believe how fast time was moving now that she was in one place. Settled, her father had said. She was now 'settled'. She didn't know what to make of that. Her days were interesting, long, but interesting. She had a natural ability for herbs and remedies, and learning the ways of the village was easier than she thought.

It was a very large town, and the healer was in constant demand; and much to Rosa's surprise, the women of the town would seek out love charms as often as remedies. On market days, she would overhear them lamenting, "If I only had a way of knowing what the future held," or "I do not understand why these dreams keep haunting me," and it made her smile. Her mother would have called this a 'target-rich environment,' her smile widened when she thought of her brother Ion, he would have said, 'a fool and his money.'

After her breakfast, she was cleaning the undercroft that stored the drying herbs when she was interrupted by one of the errand boys. She was to bring several herbs, along with her mistress's special tea set, to her where she was attending to the baker's wife. Rosa gathered the required items quickly and followed the boy. When she entered the bakery, she smiled warmly at the young girl behind the counter and slipped into the back room to find her mistress.

"Ah, Rosa, there you are, set the goods on the table and have a seat. You're to learn something today," Gerda, motioned for her to take the chair at the table next to the baker's wife. "Now, these herbs will make a tea, it is rather bland, but it's purpose is not for pleasure. You are to drink it quickly, then place the saucer upon the cup and flip the whole thing over quickly. Once you've done that, I want you to leave the room Hildie. If she is to learn, it will be easier if you aren't watching her every expression. I'll let you know what the results are." Gerda smiled to reassure Hildie, and began to crush the herbs.

Hildie, having had this done in the past was not concerned, and waited patiently without saying a word. Rosa, however, was very concerned. "What is it you wish me to do Mistress?"

"Pay attention," she quipped. "You will be doing this for me in the future, as my legs are too old for me to traipse about this town to provide this service any longer. Remember these herbs, and crush them so, mix them together, and keep the amounts even. When the water boils, pour it over the herbs and let it steep for three minutes. Understand?" Gerda asked Rosa. "While the tea is steeping, you ask the woman to think about her question. She isn't to discuss it, just think about what she wants to know until the tea is ready. Understood?"

Rosa smiled, for she understood perfectly. Her mother had taught her this skill years ago, even better, her mother had special herbs for different types of questions. Rosa wisely kept this knowledge to herself, as she had learned the hard way that Gerda didn't hold much stock in her Romani ways. Why, Rosa couldn't fathom, since every 'people' she had come across in her short life had had similar ways.

"Hildie, it's time to drink your tea." Gerda prodded Hildie, and when she complied with the saucer on top of the cup, she left to help the girl in the front room with the day's customers.

"Rosa, I want you to move the cup slowly so that it is in front of you, do not turn it or cause the leaves to shift." Gerda was pleased to see that Rosa appeared to grasp the concept. "Now remove the saucer and tell me what shapes do you see in the patterns of the leaves? Just blurt out whatever you see, we will discuss each as it comes, do not worry about what you see, just report it as it comes."

"There's a dragonfly, pointing to the west...on the opposite side, there are two trails, one shorter than the other, on the handle side there are three leaves stuck to each other, on the opposite side of the handle there is a calm," Rosa reported to Gerda, keeping her eyes on the leaves and not looking up between observations.

"Well, that's quite precise. What do you think this all means?" Gerda asked Rosa.

"The dragonfly could mean something new is coming, perhaps an opportunity? An opportunity from the West perhaps?" Rosa still didn't look at Gerda. "The two trails, one shorter, meaning there may be choices, one with less benefit than the other?"

"Go on, what do you think the three leaves mean?" her mistress prodded her.

"Perhaps that there is a third path or choice, and since the opposite side from that is level and calm, perhaps to do nothing is the third choice? That choosing to do nothing will not harm her?" At this Rosa looked into the aging healers eyes and hoped for the approval she never received from her mother.

"Well done, Rosa, I think you have the gift for reading tea leaves. It is important when you reveal your findings to the seeker that you are always sure of what you see, do not hesitate in your answers when you speak of meanings, but take your time before speaking to be sure in your mind. You must always speak with confidence, even if the news is not favorable." Gerda smiled warmly and continued, "I have noticed your touch with the herbs, you have much natural knowledge that comes from within, not from learning. I wonder what else you can learn?" Gerda didn't expect an answer and was a bit surprised when Rosa spoke up.

"Mistress, you have taught me well, and you are right, some things that you teach me I do feel as if I knew already, or that it is easy for me to grasp. But I must be honest, I think my talent lies in the mind of a person, not in the actual healing arts. I do not know how to explain my feelings, it's as if my purpose is to sooth a person's mind…" Rosa let the thought trail off as Hildie came back into the room.

"Well, does the girl show promise Gerda?" she asked.

"Aye, she does at that. We'll be leaving now my friend. Rosa, gather up my things and return to your work, I'll be along shortly." Gerda directed.

"So then Gerda, my tea leaves say I should stay the course?" Hildie smiled.

"Doesn't it always?" Gerda gave her a knowing smile and headed home towards her stillroom.

****

As autumn approached, Gerda called for Rosa to join her for the weekly trip to the market. As they walked with their empty baskets over their arms, Gerda began to question Rosa about how much she knew about tarot and the meanings of the cards. She was curious if the girl knew how to cast runes as well.

Rosa said that her mother had taught her much, but that she was out of practice since she'd been apprenticed.

"I heard word that your parents will be at the harvest fair next week, I think you should seek out your mother, see if she can help you obtain a deck or two for your own use."

"Why would I do that, if I am to be a healer, Mistress Gerda?" Rosa was afraid that she had let the healer down somehow and was in danger of being dismissed.

"I've been observing you, and I've noticed a need in our community. Not all that ails a person is in his body, sometimes his spirit is ailing. That is when I suggest a priest or holy man. But sometimes my girl, what is wrong with a person is in their mind, they are blocked by not knowing which path to take, and this causes them much distress that neither religion nor medicine can cure," she let that mull around in the girl's head for a moment before she continued. "You tried to point this out yourself this summer with the baker's wife. What I've noticed in you, child, is that you are an empath. You instinctively know what someone needs on an emotional level. I see it in everything you do."

"What does this have to do with my mother and the tarot Mistress Gerda?" Rosa nervously shifted her basket to the other arm as they drew closer to the market.

"I spoke with the Baroness last week about these concerns and she suggested we try an experiment. The Baroness would like for you to do a reading for her, and if she sees value in your work, a *non-heretical* value, she will sponsor you with a position," Gerda began.

"What kind of position?" Rosa skeptically asked.

"Soothsayer of course. She would allow for you to have your own dwelling, near mine, and she would gift you with an annual stipend. There would be specific things she will not allow you to do, as she has to appease the Church. More than that will have to come from the Baroness." Gerda nodded to the spice merchant as they passed his stall.

"I don't know what to say, Mistress, I feel as if I've failed you," Rosa began.

"Child, you have not failed me, you are simply being given an opportunity. You may always say no." Gerda chuckled and turned towards the fruit vendor as Rosa thought about what she had been told.

****

The following week, Rosa met with her mother, and as her mother listened to her story, she was filled with dread. "Momma, perhaps it is time I left the gadje and came back to you and Papa," she began.

"Tsk, Rosa. No. That is not your path any longer. Your father said your place is with them. Therefore, you are to stay 'settled,'" her mother nearly spit the word, "let me read your leaves if it eases your mind. I want you to be happy, but I must tell you, child of my heart, the tarot is not to be played with. You must respect the gifts that are bestowed upon you, but you must be wise as well. Now, give me that cup." Lala reached for the cup, only to have it knocked from her hand as Lily came running up to them, grabbing her mother's arm in her excitement. "Bah, look what you have done!" she yelled at her youngest. "You have ruined your sister's future!"

"I'm so sorry, I didn't mean too," Lily began to wail when she saw the shock on both their faces. Lily began to reach for the pieces of the broken china when she was yanked back by her arm.

"Don't touch it!" Lala hissed at Lily. "Go, find Ion, tell him his sister wants to say hello," she shooed the child in the opposite direction.

"Rosa, look at the leaves on the ground, they should be scattered all about, but they are nearly all heading north, towards the town. I cannot read your future any longer, you are lost to me," Lala nearly whispered the last part. Her eyes clouded with unshed tears.

"Momma, you will always know where to find me," Rosa began but had to stop. Her own tears choking her into silence. When she found her voice again she asked, "Momma, may I have my tarot deck? The one that Papa had painted for me?" She couldn't look up from the broken china just yet.

"Yes daughter. I'll go get them. Please, be careful while you clean your sister's mess." Lala let her hand rest on Rosa's shoulder for the briefest of moments before she headed to the wagon. Inside the wagon, Lala let the tears silently flow down her cheeks as she wrapped the deck of tarot cards in a silk cloth of her husbands, fitting, she thought, the cloth and cards were gifts from father to daughter. Then she snatched a piece of velvet she was saving and created a quick pouch with it, then wrapped a new set of runes that she had just finished inscribing as a gift from mother to daughter. Wiping her tears, she collected several selenite crystals and placed them in each of the pouches and headed back out of the wagon to find the daughter of her heart.

"Rosa, the selenite will remove any energy lingering in the decks and staves. Don't touch them until you are in your new home, by then they will be ready to respond only to your energy. Don't let anyone else touch them." Wiping the last of her tears away, Lala kissed Rosa on both cheeks. "Now, go talk to your brother and console your sister. Papa will take you back to the town when you are finished."

Lala hugged her again and left her children in the camp while she went to collect fresh water.

Rosa did as she was bid and learned from her brother that after the harvest fair, the family was leaving for warmer climates but would be back in the spring. When her father returned, he was subdued at the thought of leaving his daughter, yet again, in the town of the gadje. As they traveled, her father asked after her happiness and if life as a settled person suited her. She set his mind at ease and thanked him for the opportunity he had given her.

When they reached the dwelling of the healer, she asked her father to wait for a moment, she had something to give her mother. When she returned, she handed a carefully wrapped china tea cup and saucer to her father, "Please give this to Momma, it is to replace the one that got broken."

"You are a good daughter, but the debt is Lily's to bear, not yours," Besnik told Rosa.

"Papa, she is still a child, someday, she will owe me a cup and saucer!" Rosa chuckled as she waived her father off.

Gerda watched from the window as Rosa wiped a tear from her cheek as she watched her father pull out of sight. When Rosa came inside, she asked her if all was well.

"Aye, but I will have to obtain a new cup and saucer," she grinned ruefully at the healer.

"Well then, I suppose it is time to start charging for your services," Gerda remarked.

****

Rosa was allowed two hours a day to re-acquaint herself with the 'new tools' she would be using to aid the community. Gerda steadfastly refused to use words that spoke of a heretical belief, such as 'having the sight.' She preferred to say 'women's knowledge' and always referred to any object as a tool. It was her personal belief that it would keep the men of the community from using words like 'witch'. Everyone knew what that label would do to a woman. She was well aware that they were skating on thin ice.

As the time approached for Rosa's audience with the Baroness, her confidence grew. Every time she touched the deck her father had made for her, it warmed to her touch, and a sense of calm came over her. It gave her a connection with her family that she missed. Even the runes her mother had so painstakingly carved seemed to speak to her. Rosa was beginning to collect the herbs her mother used and was drying them with the intent to have pre-made sachets ready for when she was called on. Whenever someone came into their town from a foreign land, Rosa tried to learn all she could about their ways, being careful to never use words like 'spells.' Gerda was pleased with her progress.

The day finally arrived and Rosa was summoned to the Baroness' quarters in the castle. She brought her special herbs, the runes, and tarot to be sure she could answer the Baroness' questions using the appropriate tools. She wore her hair long and secured it with a band at her nape. She kept all ornamentation to a minimum so as to not offend, remembering what her mother used to tell her about how a gadje would mistake it as trying to be above one's class. Her father often disagreed with her mother over this, stating that it was showmanship to jingle; that the noise from the jewelry and trinkets kept the bad spirits away. Usually, her mother would roll her eyes at this point.

"A spirit is a spirit, they are neither good nor bad. Perception is in the eye of the beholder's conscience. If they deserve bad, it will be, if they have a good heart, the spirit will be benign. You know this Rosa," and so it would go until Ion would tell his mother that she needed more theatrics if she was to be successful at the next fair.

"Mama, give the Ladies what they want, the exotic, the mysterious," he would say mimicking his father.

"A gift is not to be dressed up or abused, but to be treated as sacred…" she would tell her children. These memories fortified Rosa's intention to be as true to her gifts as possible and leave the theatrics to the caravans.

When she was shown into the quarters of the Baroness, the fire was roaring and candles were on every surface, it was sweltering. The Baroness had a lap robe across her and she was shivering. Rosa felt the heat like a blast from the Smithy's forge.

"Come in child, let me have a look at you." The Baroness motioned for Rosa to come to her.

Rosa curtsied as Gerda had taught her, and waited. And waited some more.

"So, you are to be our Soothsayer." It wasn't a question, Rosa kept her tongue.

"Young, so very young…Well, let's see what the healer sees in you." The Baroness motioned with a trembling hand to the seat across from her. "Let's have a conversation shall we?"

Rosa was flushed from the stifling heat in the room, little beads of perspiration were forming on her upper lip and brow, yet she steadfastly didn't wipe it away. She didn't wish to offend.

"You're a quiet one. Tell me, child, are you afraid of me?" asked the Baroness.

"No m'Lady," Rosa spoke softly but clearly.

"You should be."

A soft smile curved Rosa's lips and she openly looked into the face of the Baroness, her smile widened as she took in the deep set violet of her eyes and recognized greatness. "Baroness, you see more than I, why am I here?"

"This town needs someone that can speak to the people on their level, set their fears to rest, give them hope when they've given up...the priests, they scare the people, forever threatening to damn their piteous souls, demanding the joy right out of them. Don't mistake me, religion has its place, but the old ways, we must not lose the old ways..." she drifted off in thought as she turned her gaze to the hearth.

"M'Lady, are you ailing?" Rosa cautiously asked.

"Aye, but not as you may think. A noblewoman could never speak to her people to sooth them in this way. The church would call it heretical. The other nobles would banish her as a witch. To have the sight…it's, not something to be admired. Most fear it, they always fear what they don't understand. When an outsider comes into a society with certain gifts, it's more easily accepted. It's explained away to the fearful as 'it's just their ways' or 'they are not like us.' Even healers must be careful. Too much secrecy of what is used in a poultice, then the fearful cry spellcraft. Knowledge is the key to overcoming fear. But that is a subject for another day."

"Baroness, how may I be of service to you today?" Rosa prompted when the Baroness was quiet for a long time.

"Ah, yes, yes. I wish to see what your Romani blood has in it. I need to know what you can do, that won't get you hung. Where your strength lies, how you can help my people. Let's start with a nice cup of tea shall we?"

Rosa noticed the cart with a lovely tea set near the hearth and rose to bring it closer. "Shall I use my herbs, or do you wish to use your own m'lady?"

"We'll use mine today. I'm sure you are aware of how to prepare it properly?"

"Aye," she paused briefly considering how to proceed with the question on her mind, decided for bluntness and dived in. "Shall I speak with you as I would the town people?"

"That would be refreshing," she said.

"Please think of the question you wish answered most. Do not speak of it to me, and while you drink your tea, think upon it. When you have finished, please place the saucer upon the cup and flip it over." Rosa spoke quickly, but her words were sure.

When Rosa looked into the cup she was overcome with visions of a battle, crosses on one side and mounds on the other, two figures were standing among the mounds. Rosa's hands were shaking as she set the cup back down and looked at the Baroness sharply. "You know this already?"

"And now, so do you, my young friend. The question is, are you the other figure standing with me?"

Rosa didn't answer, but she opened her pouch and removed the staves carved by her mother, she spoke silently to them, mouthing the words but not making a sound. When she read them, she looked grim.

"So your runes confirm it then," the Baroness spoke as if she were pleased.

"Do you want the tarot read on this topic or another m'lady," Rosa tried to keep her concern out of her voice, she was visibly sweating now.

"I approve of the way you do your casting of runes. There is no silliness to it, nothing heretical. I'm glad you don't do what they do in the caravans, killing chickens and the such. I would suggest however that you explain what each rune says beforehand so that the people of this town will not think you inventive."

Rosa nodded her head, "Aye, m'lady. I shall remember to do that in the future."

"I assume you have your own deck?" The Baroness asked.

As she opened another pouch, she stroked the crystal that was inside, whether for strength or out of habit, Rosa didn't know.

"Beautiful, may I?" the Baroness reached for the deck.

"No! I'm sorry Baroness, but no one can touch my deck, it will disturb the energies held within," Rosa was startled at her own response.

"I understand, it's good you know and are respectful of the gift. I'm glad you didn't let me touch it. You must be firm with the people, yet gentle, explain the why's so the church won't claim heretic."

"Baroness, you know how to read the cards?" Rosa was just confirming this knowledge, not really asking. "Then shall I do a three or five card spread?"

"Oh let's keep it simple today, shall we? Let's do a three and see if my question needs further clarification." The Baroness removed the lap robe and proceeded to work her way around the room blowing out candles until only the one on the table in front of Rosa was left burning. "Ah, much better, suddenly, I feel the chill has left my bones," she smiled, rubbed her hands together, then sat down directly across from Rosa with her palms face down on the table. "Shall we begin?"

Rosa shuffled the cards thrice, then placed three cards face down in a row as the Baroness closed her eyes and thought about what she wanted answered. Rosa flipped the first card over, going from left to right. "Ace of Swords, right side up. King of Cups, right side up. Knight of Cups. Right side up." Rosa took a cleansing breath.

"Why did you not explain what the cards meant as they were revealed?" The Baroness questioned.

"It is useless Baroness unless you have the entire story, you do not know what the cards mean. The meaning can change depending upon whether they are right side up or reversed. The order of the cards matters…where the cards lay in conjunction with each other matter. It is unwise m'lady to speak before the story is known." Rosa hoped she answered correctly.

"Ah, my child, the healer was correct. You are wiser than your years. Your mother taught you well. Now, tell me what this story says?"

"The Ace of Swords, new beginnings-opportunities, Swords themselves relate to the Air or Fire-challenges, intellect or ways of thinking. The other two cards are Cups, which relate to the heart. Water, emotions, creativity and relationships. The King of Cups then signifies maturity, organization, and control. The Knight of Cups speaks of focus, perhaps even fanatical or fast moving."

"Go on," the Baroness prompted, "put it together in a story now."

Rosa gently touched the Ace of Swords and began speaking, moving her fingers over each card in turn, "You seek the truth of the situation, you wish to know if the opportunity you seek will change the ways the people think. You are fortunate, powerful and wise, yet you feel restless as if something is missing. You wish to move ahead quickly and appease this feeling of something lacking. Be careful Baroness, that you do not focus so much on this wish for a soothsayer, that you neglect your people's other needs."

"Clever girl."

"It is the cards m'lady."

"Of course, it is. You are an empath as well, this helps you ferret out what the questioner really wants to know. This just might work after all," the Baroness strummed her fingers on the table deep in thought as Rosa collected her tools.

*****

True to her word, the Baroness set Rosa up in her own cottage near the healer and as the years passed the community relied on her more and more. She was happy enough with her 'settled' life, even though she missed her family deeply. They came through her town less and less frequently now. Lily was grown and was truly a star as her father always called her, she had the showmanship their brother Ion was always pushing his mother to exhibit and Lala became the crone in truth. Beznik missed his settled child, but his life was for travel.

The last time Rosa ever saw her sister Lily, it was not in person. Rosa had come home from visiting the Baroness, now aged and bedridden, and found a package on her hearthstone. When she opened it, it was a beautiful tea cup and saucer, embellished with hand painted roses. The china was so fine, you could see the shadow of your fingers through it, there was no card enclosed, but Rosa knew it was from her sister. When she turned the saucer over, there in the center, was a lovely hand painted Lily.

Contributors

Vanessa Essler Carlson

Vanessa is an eclectic storyteller and daydreamer currently carving out her creative niche in an ever-changing tide of literature. Residing in the strawberry sunsets of Northern Arizona with her husband and two young daughters, she is a freelance writer and recent college graduate having earned a Bachelor's degree in Creative Writing and English. She has won the Founders Award for her fiction from the Professional Writers of Prescott and her work has appeared in Z-Composition.

Sammi Cox

Sammi Cox lives in the UK and spends her time writing and making things. She has been interested in history, archeology, and the natural world since she was a child. However, it is tales of myth, magic and folklore that have captured her heart, and where she finds the greatest inspiration.

Evelyn M. Zimmer

Evelyn began her writing career in the second half of her life. While she has always had a love affair with the written word, it wasn't until now that she has had the time to dedicate herself to her passion. In her spare time, she enjoys various activities with her friends and visiting her family across the States.

She lives in her family home in Michigan with her husband Paul and the newest addition to their family, a Shih-Tzu named Leo.

E.W. Farnsworth

E.W. lives and writes in Arizona. Over fifty of E.W.'s short stories were published in 2015. His collected western stories, spy stories, John Fulghum Mysteries and an Anderson romance/thriller also appeared in 2015. Bitcoin Fandango, his mystery/thriller about combating Bitcoin crimes, appeared in March 2015. For more information about E.W., see his website at **www.ewfarnsworth.com.**

Additional Anthologies from Zimbell House Publishing

Reflections: Michigan 2015
Reflections: Seasons 2015
The Fairy Tale Whisperer
Puppy Love: 2015
The Mysteries of Suspense
Garden of the Goddesses
Elemental Foundations
Romantic Morsels
The Steam Chronicles
Pagan
Tales from the Grave
The Adventures of Pirates
Curse of the Tomb Seekers

New Releases Coming Soon from Zimbell House Publishing

Dark Monsters
On a Dark and Snowy Night
Where Cowboys Roam
The Key

How to Thank a Contributor

Dear Reader,

Everyone at Zimbell House Publishing would like to thank you for reading *Travelers*. If you would like to thank a particular contributor, the best way is to leave a review for them. You may do so by leaving one on our Goodreads page, under the *Travelers* title, by clicking the link below:

http://www.goodreads.com/ZimbellHousePublishing

and be sure to mention the contributor directly.

Why leave a review? Reviews help budding authors build their credibility in the book industry. By posting a review on Goodreads, you help other readers find new authors they may wish to follow, and you never know, your review may end up on an author's website one day.

Friend us on Goodreads:
https://www.goodreads.com/ZimbellHousePublishing
Visit our website:
http://www.ZimbellHousePublishing.com
Follow us on Twitter:
http://twitter.com/ZimbellHousePub